When Lindsay Collins cleared her throat, Joe Rossetti straightened. What was he doing, losing his focus like that?

"Here, let me buzz you back," Clara, the department's secretary, said. "You can have a private conversation at one of the desks in the squad room. I'm sure Trooper Rossetti will help you in any way he can." Clara's lips twitched as she reached for a button to the side of her desk to let Lindsay in. Always the matchmaker.

Joe took a deep breath. Couldn't the people around this post mind their own business just once? He wasn't used to failure, either, and Lindsay Collins represented the biggest failure of his career so far. She stepped through the door to the left of the counter with the aid of a tortoiseshell cane.

Like it or not, he had to face her. And she would want answers that he wasn't prepared to give.

Books by Dana Corbit

Love Inspired

A Blessed Life
An Honest Life
A New Life
A Family for Christmas
  "Child in a Manger"
On the Doorstep
Christmas in the Air
  "Season of Hope"
A Hickory Ridge Christmas
Little Miss Matchmaker
Homecoming at Hickory Ridge
*An Unexpected Match
*His Christmas Bride
*Wedding Cake Wishes
Safe in His Arms

*Wedding Bell Blessings

DANA CORBIT

started telling "people stories" at about the same time she started forming words. So it came as no surprise when the Indiana native chose a career in journalism. As an award-winning newspaper reporter and features editor, she had the opportunity to share wonderful true-life stories with her readers. She left the workforce to be a homemaker, but the stories came home with her as she discovered the joy of writing fiction. The winner of the 2007 Holt Medallion competition for novel writing, Dana feels blessed to share the stories of her heart with readers.

Dana lives in southeast Michigan, where she balances the make-believe realm of her characters with her equally exciting real-life world as a wife, carpool coordinator for three athletic daughters and food supplier for two disinterested felines.

Safe in His Arms
Dana Corbit

Love Inspired

Recycling programs for this product may not exist in your area.

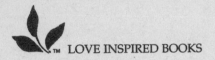

LOVE INSPIRED BOOKS

ISBN-13: 978-0-373-81573-9

SAFE IN HIS ARMS

www.LoveInspiredBooks.com

Printed in U.S.A.

He will feed his flock like a shepherd,
he will gather the lambs in his arms,
he will carry them in his bosom,
and gently lead those that are with young.
—*Isaiah* 40:11

To my very own hero, Randy…
my partner, my best friend. Thank you for cooking
more than your share of family dinners, being
a great tag-team carpool dad and pretending to
understand my roller coaster ride of a creative
process as I tell my stories. Thanks to my friends,
Cindy Thomas, who helped me finish this book
by offering your cottage as a writing cave, and
Dr. Celia D'Errico, D.O., who helped make the
medical portion of this story believable.

Also, a special thank you to Michigan State Police
Trooper Christopher Grace for opening his world
and providing inspiration for the character of
Joe Rossetti. Any mistakes in the story are my own.

Chapter One

Hot afternoons and hot heads made for some blistering combinations on the roadways, as far as Joe Rossetti was concerned. So, with the steamiest July day so far in the forecast, his anxiety was already building, and he wasn't out on patrol yet.

"Hey, Trooper Rossetti."

Joe stopped just as he pushed open the heavy steel door at the Michigan State Police, Brighton Post, and a wall of humidity reached out to steal his breath.

He glanced back over his shoulder. "Yes, Lieutenant?"

"Someone's out there to see you." Lieutenant Matt Dawson paused on the path to his office and looked at Joe over the top of the glasses he probably only wore to make him look older. He indicated the radio room with a tilt of his head.

Joe groaned under his breath, but he nodded and let the door close again. "Be right there."

Patting along his black duty belt and brushing a hand over his holstered weapon to make sure everything was in place, he straightened his shoulders and headed to the radio room that separated the visitor area from the squad room.

A little excitement to start his day. Strange, how he used to secretly hope for diversions to break up a shift's monotony. Nowadays he preferred to pull eight uneventful hours patrolling the highways of Detroit's western suburbs. To him, *excitement* had come to mean having to tell another set of parents that their kid was never coming home.

"Are you Trooper Rossetti?"

The pretty redhead peering at him from across the counter didn't strike him as familiar, but that didn't surprise him. He came across a lot of people every day, more out in the community than he'd ever cuffed and put in his patrol car.

"That's me. May I help you?"

She settled something beneath the ledge and leaned against it, gripping her hands together on the countertop. "You won't remember me...."

Strange, but as soon as she'd said it, Joe had the unsettling sense that he *did* remember her. Through his work, he'd learned to trust his instincts, so he took a good look at her. Something did look familiar, but he couldn't pinpoint it. Was it her mass of red hair, with all of the colors of fire in it, her almost translucent skin, or the dusting of freckles across her nose? When she looked up at him again, though, he realized that it was none of those things that tickled at the fringes of his memory.

It was her eyes. The same pale blue eyes that had filled his nightmares for the last six months. The eyes that had begged him for the kind of help he couldn't give. At once a memory of the accident and the fire covered his thoughts like a shower of metal fragments and charred upholstery, as his failed attempt to complete a one-officer rescue burned through his memory. A bungled job of protecting and serving.

Joe blinked but couldn't look away from her. He felt trapped by the intensity of her stare, convicted by the accusation in it. Recognition had to be written all over his face, but she must have missed it, because she cleared her throat and tried again.

"I'm sorry. I'm really nervous. My name is Lindsay Collins, and I…"

It was all he could do to avoid saying "I know who you are." He could even fill in the details. Age twenty-eight. A Wixom address. She was the woman he'd hovered over for hours as she'd lay in that hospital bed, drifting in and out of consciousness. Staying with a victim too long to avoid becoming personally involved in the tragedy was a mistake but far from the only one he'd made that night. All of the mistakes demonstrated how he'd forfeited his professional distance and his edge as a police officer—all on one stormy night.

Had he consciously chosen which of the victims would survive when he'd pulled the driver out of the car, even as she'd begged him to help her unconscious sister first? Had he really believed that he had time to assist both victims before the car burst into flames, or had his oversize ego made him think he could pull off some superhuman feat? Was he to blame for a woman's death?

The poem. He swallowed, remembering yet another mistake he'd made the night of the accident. It was just a poem about God that a friend had included inside his birthday card last February. Joe didn't even know why he'd started carrying it around inside his trooper's hat. If someone had told him that one day he would pass it along to someone in crisis, he would have laughed out loud. He wasn't even one of those *God* people.

And then that night he'd done it. Lindsay Collins had looked so alone, lying in that hospital bed. Even her parents were down the hall on their cell phones, notifying relatives and preparing for a funeral. Joe had felt so helpless, watching her, that before he'd thought better of it he'd pulled the piece of paper out of his hat and tucked it in her hands. As if some poem that told her she was a child of God could make up for all she'd lost that night. As if anything could.

When Lindsay cleared her throat, Joe straightened. What was he doing, losing his focus like that?

"Here, let me buzz you back," Clara Morrison, the secretary, said. "You can have a private conversation at one of the desks in the squad room."

Clara, the youngest sixty-year-old Joe knew, and the go-to gal for Brighton Post gossip, pretended to miss it when Joe shook his head. She turned back to the redhead.

"I'm sure Trooper Rossetti will help you in any way he can." Clara's lips twitched as she reached for a button at the side of her desk.

Joe took a deep breath. Couldn't the people around this post mind their own business just once? Nothing usually ruffled him, but he was more than unsettled lately. He wasn't used to failure either, and Lindsay Collins represented the biggest failure of his career so far.

"Thank you."

Lindsay bent to retrieve the item she'd rested below the counter and shifted when she heard the buzz. She stepped through the door with the aid of a tortoiseshell cane.

"Right this way," he said, covering his surprise. He started toward one of the open desks in the squad room, but had to slow himself to her pace. He didn't realize he was staring at her cane until she waved it off the floor.

"Oh, this? The doctors said I won't always need it, but I'm still healing. Broken pelvis and broken right femur. I crushed my whole hip socket joint. It's taken a while to recover."

"Sometimes it does take a while."

He already knew about the two months she'd spent at Meadows Rehabilitation Center, thanks to updates from his nurse friends. He could only imagine how tough her recovery had been, given the extent of her injuries. She'd had so much internal bleeding from the pelvis fracture, that the doctors said she was lucky to have survived.

Just as they reached the desk, the door to the locker room swung wide and Trooper Angela Vincent emerged in uniform, still adjusting the knot on her light blue tie. Trooper Garrett Taylor pushed through the opposite door, brushing his fingers across his silver badge, as if to make sure it was straight. Neither bothered hiding their curiosity about the woman who maneuvered herself into a chair and propped her cane next to it.

So much for life in a fishbowl. Joe almost wished he'd led her into the interview room instead, but then his coworkers would have been watching them through the one-way glass window.

As he sat in the seat opposite hers, Joe studied the woman he'd only seen one time before, on what had to be the worst day of her life. Her hair was tied back, not flowing past her shoulders the way it had been the night of the accident. Not matted with blood. He couldn't help but notice the small pink scars just beneath her jawline, and another that peeked out from the ruffled edge of her white, sleeveless blouse.

Even with those tiny imperfections, Lindsay Collins was one of the prettiest women he'd ever seen. And one of the saddest. Those blue eyes had an empty quality to them, like a tranquil swimming pool where no one swam anymore.

"Now, how may I help you?"

She pressed her full red lips together and then spoke. "I saw your name on the report for the auto accident I was involved in six months ago."

Joe cleared his throat. "I'm sorry. I do a lot of accident reports."

He hated pretending he couldn't remember, but he doubted it would be helpful to tell her that, though many accident reports blurred together, he could still see hers in bold print.

"This one involved a fire and two fatalities, a man and a woman."

Joe could only nod. He might have told her that he'd investigated half a dozen fatalities in the past year—victims related only by the stretch of highway where their lives met with tragic ends—but she set a copy of the police report on the desk in front of him. Staring down at it for several seconds, he finally picked it up.

"I remember."

"You do?"

The strange sound of her voice had him watching her more carefully. Maybe she couldn't picture that awful scene as clearly as he could.

"I was the first responder."

She turned her head to the side, blinking a few times. When she looked back at him, her lashes were damp.

"I can't remember anything about the accident," she admitted. She glanced down at the report, dragging her front teeth over her bottom lip. "The woman who died...Delia Banks...was my sister."

He already knew that, too, but he didn't tell her so, as the raw sound of her voice cut through the detachment he was trying so hard to maintain. But then he'd failed at keeping a personal distance in this case from the moment he'd arrived on the scene.

"I'm sorry for your loss."

He hated to offer her platitudes, but he refused to tell her he was sorry she couldn't remember the accident. He wouldn't wish pictures like that to be painted on anyone's memory, in a gruesome palette of blood and twisted metal. Her subconscious had taken pity on her, allowing her to forget things that would be too hard to bear.

"Were you the only officer on the scene?"

"No, just the first. Why do you ask?" He tried to look calm, resting his forearms on the edge of the desk, but his thoughts were spinning. Was she putting together information for a lawsuit? Sure, he'd failed to get both women out of the vehicle before it burst into flames, but had he given anyone grounds to sue?

"My sister...she was my best friend."

Lindsay brushed her index finger reflexively along the line of a jagged, pink scar on the back of her left hand. Probably from the glass. She didn't seem to be speaking to him, so Joe didn't try to answer. What would he say? He'd already told her he was sorry for her loss. He just hadn't said how much.

"We were having the best day," she continued. "We just didn't realize it would be our last one together."

"I really am sorry."

The words sounded empty to him. Impotent. As incapable of providing comfort as those that had been spoken on that day so long ago, when he'd worn his first grown-up suit, with a tie that strangled his tiny neck. Joe wiped a sweaty hand on his blue uniform trousers, leaving a mark.

He refused to allow his thoughts to travel that

far back through history, especially when he was beginning to wonder just what Lindsay Collins wanted from her visit. Complaints were easier to handle. He would try tactful discussion first, and if that didn't work, he had his sergeant for backup. But what was he supposed to do now? He'd never been good with women when they cried. If Lindsay started, he might say anything to get her to stop.

"I wish there was something I could do," he began, not knowing what else to say.

"There is something." She looked up from the desk, an intensity that had been missing before now filling her eyes. "You could answer a few questions for me about that day. Fill in some of the blanks."

"Are you sure you want to know?"

Her gaze narrowed at him. "Of course I am."

Was it reflex or just plain cowardice that made him look at his watch then? So much for the Rossetti legacy of bravery on the force. Still, he had a job to do, and he already should have been out on patrol, discouraging drivers from turning Interstate 96 into the Autobahn.

"I'm late right now, but we could set up an appointment…" He let his words trail away as he gestured toward the radio room.

"That's fine." With jerky movements, she stood and grabbed her cane for balance. "But if it wouldn't be too much trouble, could I ask just one question now?"

"Okay."

Technically, she was already asking one, and another would make it two. Joe didn't point that out, but he didn't sit again, either. Instead, he reached out a hand to her, signaling that their meeting was ending.

Lindsay traded the cane to her left hand and leaned on it for balance as they shook hands. *Small. Fragile.* She pulled her hand away quickly, as if she refused to let him see her vulnerability, and she trapped him in her steady gaze. At a willowy five-feet-nine, she barely had to tilt her head up to look him in the eye.

He cleared his throat. "Your question?"

Her bravado must have faltered, because she stared at her hands before looking up at him again.

"Why did you save me instead of her?"

Lindsay stared out the window at the patrol car that scattered gravel as it raced from the parking lot, its red light spinning and its siren blaring. From the look on Trooper Rossetti's face when she'd asked the question, she wondered if he would have run from the squad room if his radio hadn't beeped right then, giving him an excuse to go.

"Sorry about that," the front-desk lady who'd buzzed her in earlier said now that Lindsay was out front again. "You never know when a call is going to come in."

"Oh, no problem."

She glanced out the window to the parking lot again. Maybe it hadn't been the best question to ask first—she should have warmed up to it—but Trooper Rossetti had looked as shocked as he might have if she'd pulled a gun on him. The reaction was extreme. Was there something about the night of the accident that he didn't want to tell her?

"I'm Clara Morrison. I can help you." The woman glanced down at her desktop computer and started clicking through several screens. "Now, Miss Collins, Trooper Rossetti said you wanted to set up an appointment to speak with him further. When would be best for you?"

"Later today?"

Clara grinned, obviously getting the wrong idea about why Lindsay might want an appointment with the young police officer. She wanted to clear that up right away.

"I'm only here about a traffic accident he investigated."

"Of course." As Clara turned back to the screen, the side of her mouth lifted.

Lindsay couldn't blame the woman for not buying her story. Even as focused as she'd been on getting him to answer her questions, she'd still had her eyes open when she'd met Trooper Rossetti. No woman with her eyes open could have failed to notice his shiny, dark brown eyes and heavy fringe of even darker lashes. And that perfectly formed mouth and straight white teeth would have been hard to miss.

Guys like him were hired to play cops on TV, not to strap on the holster and dodge bullets for real. Delia would have called him "a hunk," and Lindsay would have been too awkward around him to even speak, if this had been a social situation. It wasn't.

"My sister died in that accident."

Immediately, Lindsay was sorry for being so blunt, and she felt even guiltier when the woman glanced over at her with a compassionate look on her face.

"I'm so sorry."

"I'm sorry, too. I shouldn't have said it that way." She shook her head. "I just can't recall much about that day, and I'd hoped that Trooper Rossetti could fill in some of the details."

"I'm sure he'll try." Clara turned back to the computer, scanning down through an appointment schedule. "How about at thirteen hundred—one o'clock—tomorrow?"

Not the best time, but Lindsay would try to work with it. "So I'll meet him here?"

Clara nodded and then turned back to her screen. "I'll get a message out to him."

"Thanks." Lindsay tucked the papers she'd brought with her back into her purse and settled it on her shoulder. Then, retrieving her cane, she started toward the door.

"Miss Collins," Clara called after her and waited until she looked back at her. "Have you ever considered that you might be better off *not* remembering every detail of your accident? That knowing might only cause more pain?"

"Yes, I've thought about that. I've been thinking about that for the past six months." Lindsay chewed the side of her lower lip and then straightened and nodded. She could do this; she owed it to Delia. She would get this right for her sake. "And I still want to know."

Chapter Two

Joe leaned against the counter in the radio room, crossing his arms and his ankles and putting on his best frown. He didn't know why he bothered trying to look annoyed when Clara was so obviously ignoring him as she tapped away on her keyboard.

"Why did you set this up on my day off, anyway?"

Her shoulder lifted and dropped, but she didn't turn back to him. "What else did you have to do this afternoon?"

"I'm sure I could have found something."

Joe glanced down at his khaki shorts and striped polo shirt as he stepped out into the visitor area. He felt out of place without his uniform and the air of authority that came with it. The idea of meeting with Lindsay Collins today didn't sit well with him, but he had no one to blame but himself for agreeing to it. He had to admit, though, that he would have agreed to anything yesterday to avoid the question Lindsay had asked him. Even to delay it.

"Pretty, isn't she?"

"I hadn't noticed." Or tried not to. And failed.

"You noticed, all right. It's about time you started noticing again. At thirty-four, you—"

"If you're about to mention my biological clock, you can stop right there. Wrong gender."

"You said it. I didn't."

The door opened before he could tell Clara to stay out of his personal life. Lindsay started inside, her hair pulled back into a long ponytail, her eyes hidden behind dark sunglasses. Effortless beauty. Julianne Moore with all that red hair and none of the paparazzi.

Joe cleared his throat and squashed those thoughts at the same time. If those musings weren't signals that he should cancel this meeting, then he didn't know what was. He needed to establish a professional distance with this woman, where he'd failed the night of the accident. He would tell her that everything he knew was already in the police report and send her on her way. Simple, right? Right.

Lindsay was leaning heavily on her cane and appeared to be struggling with the door, so he stepped over and pushed it wide for her. The source of her struggle was attached to her other hand: a preschool-age girl who stared up at him with eyes as pale blue as Lindsay's.

"Hi, Trooper Rossetti." Pulling off her sunglasses, Lindsay gestured with a tilt of her head to the child beside her. "This is Emma."

Joe looked back and forth between them, searching for other similar traits. From the police report, he'd figured Lindsay was single. He didn't recall anything about her having a daughter and couldn't remember having seen a child-safety seat in the back of the crushed car. And yet, while the girl's dark, curly ponytails couldn't have been more opposite from Lindsay's fiery mane, those eyes connected the two of them.

He crouched in front of the child. "Hello, Emma. My name is Trooper Rossetti."

"Hi." Emma dipped her head, staring out at him from beneath her bangs.

"How old are you?"

She grinned bashfully and held up three fingers.

"Well, then you're a big girl."

Joe grinned first at the woman and then at the child. So much for his tough-cop image. Little girls like his own niece had always been able to turn him to mush. Sending Lindsay and her tough questions away would be hard enough. Adding a cute kid to the equation just wasn't fair.

Lindsay cleared her throat. "I almost didn't recognize you out of uniform."

"It's my day off," he told her as he came to his feet.

"I'm sorry. I didn't realize." Lindsay's gaze darted to the woman who'd scheduled the appointment and then back to him. "If you want to do this another day…"

She was giving him an out, and he was tempted to take it. "Maybe you and your daughter—"

"Niece." She lowered her voice. "She is Delia's daughter. Her name is Emma Banks."

"Oh." Joe swallowed. He hadn't seen that one coming. And the fact that he hadn't considered it was another sign that he wasn't at the top of his game.

"Delia made me Emma's guardian."

That sad, empty look entered her eyes again. Pressing her lips together, as if to settle her emotions, she smiled at the child. Emma had released her hand and was scrambling into a waiting-area chair.

"Emma, be careful. You're going to get hurt."

The child barely glanced back at her aunt before righting her backside in the chair and reaching for a brochure on the table next to her. She pretended to read the document on Michigan's concealed-weapon permit laws, but she held it upside down.

"Honey, why don't you put that back?"

"No." Emma clutched the brochure to her chest.

"She can have that one," Joe said.

Lindsay smiled, appearing relieved to skip the battle. "She's a great kid...usually."

"You're lucky to have each other," he said, when nothing else better came to mind.

He couldn't help glancing again at Emma. The girl had lost her mother, a reality that no child should have to experience, and a horror that he knew firsthand. At least he could remember a few things about his own mother. Her sweet spirit. Her soft hair. Emma wouldn't remember her mother at all, except through pictures and through the stories relatives like Lindsay would tell her.

A lump formed in his throat as he looked back to Lindsay, who was watching her niece, as well. Lindsay's eyes were moist.

Joe knew he'd lost. Whether or not he was at fault for the accident, he couldn't help feeling partially responsible for Emma losing her mother and for Lindsay being saddled with the responsibility of a child. The least he could do was to answer a few uncomfortable questions for them.

"How about we get out of here? There's a park in New Hudson where Emma can play while I answer your questions."

"Park?" Emma's eyes lit up, and she was already climbing down from the chair.

"It's settled then," he said.

Lindsay looked back to him and smiled. Her smile was so potent, so mesmerizing, that Joe had to turn away to keep from gawking at her.

That he happened to turn toward Clara, who was watching him instead of her computer screen, was downright unfortunate. She gave him a knowing smile. He frowned. Clara had no idea what situation she was messing with.

"See you tomorrow, Clara," Joe called out, as he opened the door for Lindsay and Emma.

"Park! Park!" the child called out.

With Lindsay balancing on her cane and holding Emma's hand, it was slow going, but they finally reached the white four-door in one of the visitor spaces.

"Do you mean the park built on the old landfill?" she asked, as she opened the left rear door.

"That's the one. James Atchison Memorial Park."

He waited until she'd buckled the child in her car seat and climbed into her car before he jogged around the building to the lot where troopers parked their personal vehicles. He climbed into his quad-cab pickup, relieved to be inside, even if the interior was smoldering.

"You owe them this much," he whispered to the inside walls of the truck cab.

Why did you save me instead of her? Her question reverberated through his thoughts again, as dread made his limbs feel heavy. How was he supposed to answer that? But he would answer it and her other questions, telling her as much of the truth as he could.

Only after he'd answered Lindsay's questions and put her and her niece out of his life would he be able to tuck away his own questions about his instincts on the job and finally get his edge back. He had to reclaim it somehow—soon—before he lost his job or got himself or someone else killed.

"Push me again, Trooper Joe."

"Okay, but only one last time, Miss Emma," he said. "Then we need to take a break."

His muscled arms flexing against the fabric of his polo shirt, Joe pushed the swing. This time Emma went so high that the swing jerked for a weightless moment at the top before gliding back down again. Instead of crying like Lindsay thought she might, Emma laughed with that delighted sound that only children can make.

"Do it again. Do it again," Emma called out.

"Okay, but just one…more…time."

The two of them had been playing like this for half an hour, and Lindsay didn't see them stopping anytime soon. So much for the trooper answering questions. She shouldn't have been surprised he was avoiding it, when he had appeared ready to cancel their meeting entirely until he'd learned that Emma was Delia's daughter.

He'd only changed his mind because of Emma. Was it that obvious, even to a stranger, that Lindsay wouldn't be a good guardian? She already had enough uncertainties herself, without having others question her. Why did Emma take to Joe so easily, even giving him a nickname after knowing him for ten minutes, when everything had been a struggle for Lindsay? She could barely get her niece to eat her vegetables or brush her teeth. Lindsay was the woman here. Where was the maternal instinct that was supposed to kick in when she needed it?

At least they were having fun, Lindsay decided, as she sat on a blanket, watching from beneath one of the park's few shade trees. And she couldn't have kept up with Emma's running, anyway. Running was a part of a whole other life for Lindsay…the one before the accident.

Joe finally jogged up to the blanket, carrying Emma piggyback. "I think we're both ready for a nap."

"You must be," Lindsay agreed, shifting, so her stiff leg would be in a more comfortable position.

But Emma shook her head. "I don't want a nap."

Joe lowered Emma to the ground and then he dropped on his knees on the blanket. When he was seated, with his legs stretched out and crossing his ankles, Emma settled next to him, sitting in the same position.

"Whew, it's hot out here." Joe brushed his hand back through his light brown hair that he wore trimmed close on the sides, but slightly longer on top. On his day off, he'd put a little gel in it.

"Whew." Emma copied his move, brushing back her bangs.

"You've got a little mimic there."

Joe only smiled. The last thing Lindsay would have expected was for a tough police officer to be good with kids. But then, Trooper Rossetti was nothing if not a contradiction, with his towering linebacker build and a face that could have landed him on the cover of *GQ*.

"Here. I brought these." Lindsay reached into her bag and handed them juice boxes. She was pleased with herself that she'd remembered those and some animal crackers. At least she had the snack-preparedness part of being a guardian down.

"Thanks." He helped Emma pop her straw through the hole in her box and started on his own.

By the time that both boxes were empty, Emma was already snuggling down on the blanket, her lids heavy.

"Somebody needs a nap after all," Joe whispered. For a few minutes, Joe sat brushing Emma's sweaty bangs back from her face with his finger-tips in a tender move that again didn't fit with the image of a tough police officer. Lindsay couldn't help but watch as his fingers continued their mesmerizing, gentle brushing.

She wasn't really imagining what it would feel like if he were brushing her hair like that, was she? Lindsay pushed away the thought as ridiculous.

"Is she asleep?"

At Joe's whispered words, she started, her face feeling warm. Joe gestured toward Emma.

"Well, is she?"

She nodded. "You're really good with kids."

"I have a niece, too. Kelsey's thirteen now, and completely spoiled. Mostly by me." He smiled down at Emma, as if remembering his niece at that age. "I used to baby-sit while my brother and sister-in-law took night classes."

He probably thought Lindsay hadn't baby-sat enough before being named Emma's guardian, but he didn't say so.

Finally, Joe looked up again. "Well, you wanted to ask me some questions."

He straightened, as if preparing himself for an onslaught. Lindsay couldn't blame him. She'd hit him with the toughest question yesterday.

She shifted again because her leg was already getting stiff. "It's just that it's killing me, having this blank spot in my memory. And don't tell me I'm better off not knowing. Everyone says that."

"Okay. I won't." He took a deep breath and began. "It was a rainy January instead of a snowy one, and it was pouring that night. The traffic was moving too fast and—"

She kept nodding her head until he paused, cocking his head to the side. Then she broke in.

"Those are the things you put in the police report. I want to know the things you didn't put in it."

He watched her in a measuring gaze, as if trying to decide if she could handle the truth. Could she? What if he told her that the accident was her fault? She'd suspected it, but that was different than hearing it spoken aloud.

"Okay. The scene was a mess. It was raining so hard that I was nearly on top of it before I saw it. Twisted, smoking metal was everywhere. Your car rolled and came to rest backward in the ditch."

He paused, perhaps hoping she would tell him it was enough, but she only nodded for him to continue. She tried to picture the scene as he described it, but the images refused to come together in her thoughts.

"The semi driver made a mistake passing. A fatal one." He traced a finger along the hemmed edge of the blanket as he spoke. "I called for backup and then rushed to the truck. After I determined the driver was a K— Uh, sorry, that means 'killed.' Well, after that, I went to the car."

"Delia was still alive, right?"

He cleared his throat. "There was a pulse."

"You know what I want to know, then. Why me?" She hated that her voice cracked when she asked, that her need to know had knotted her insides.

Joe brushed his palms on the legs of his cargo shorts. "From initial examination, I determined that the passenger's injuries were more serious than the driver's. The passenger was also unconscious. Since I was expecting backup, and I didn't want to cause the victim further injury if I could avoid it, I assisted the driver first. I was hoping for a quick response from the EMTs."

Lindsay wondered if he realized how strange his voice sounded, as if he was testifying in court instead of just filling her in on what happened the night of the accident. As a police officer, he had to know how to read body language to determine whether suspects might be lying. She might not have his level of training, but even she had to question the pointed way he was avoiding meeting her gaze. What wasn't he telling her?

"But it didn't turn out as you'd hoped, did it?" she asked him, when he didn't say more.

"No, it didn't." He didn't look up as he said it.

"After assisting the first victim to safety near the underpass, I started back for the second victim."

"You were too late." She'd known this all along, so why did it create so much of an ache inside her now?

"I was too late."

His softly spoken words carried the finality of a judge handing down a death sentence. Wasn't that what he'd given her sister when he'd chosen not to pull her from the car first? No. Of course not. She wasn't being fair, but she couldn't help it. Whether she'd had serious injuries or not, he hadn't even given Delia a *chance* to survive. No matter how rational his reasons, he had chosen between Lindsay's life and her sister's. She couldn't help but wonder if he'd made the wrong choice.

"The car burst into flames," Joe continued. "I sprinted back to it, but I couldn't get past the heat."

Lindsay nodded to let him know she'd heard him, even though his words made her feel as raw as she had right after the accident, when she wore her wounds on the outside as well as the inside.

Joe sat in a stiff pose, as if bracing himself for more questions. She wanted to ask him some, too. Like why he hadn't realized that the car would burst into flames and why he hadn't at least given Delia a chance by pulling her out first. But the points were moot, the consequences devastating.

Still, Joe had put himself in danger, at least attempting to save them both, and he deserved her gratitude, even if she didn't understand his decisions.

"Thank you—" she paused as each word caused a fresh pinprick to her heart, but she finally forced out "—for saving me." She brushed thumbs along her lash lines, catching tears before they could fall.

"You're welcome." Color stained his cheeks, and he watched the child next to him, instead of looking at Lindsay. "I was just doing my job."

"Well, thanks for doing your job," she said. "Come to think of it, with the extent of *my* injuries, how were you able to walk me to safety?"

"I didn't help you walk." He drew his brows together and watched her, seeming surprised she hadn't figured out that answer herself. "I carried you."

Lindsay stared at him, her jaw slack. Maybe she couldn't remember the accident, but she should have realized she never could have walked away from that car, even with help. But she was having trouble digesting that the handsome police officer had carried her.

"I really shouldn't have moved you," he said with a shrug. "It could have made your injuries worse. I thought your leg might be broken, but I didn't know about the pelvis break."

"My parents told me that I was in critical condition that first day or so."

He nodded and glanced down again at the child, who had shifted and was using his leg as a pillow.

"So," he began, when he looked up again, "how are you adapting to instant motherhood?"

Lindsay blinked. As much as she didn't want to talk about her injuries anymore, she hadn't expected him to ask about that. "Oh. We're okay. It's a transition…for both of us, but we're learning together."

She wished she could stop there. Should have. But she heard herself droning on anyway. "We're going to be great. I just know it. I fixed up the second bedroom in my condo for her, and…"

At his smile, she finally let her words trail away.

"It's got to be tough."

"I never expected to struggle this much."

"Parents struggle, even those who have their kids from birth."

"Emma doesn't even live with me full-time yet."

He lifted a brow. "What do you mean?"

"After the accident, Mom and Dad took care of Emma while I was in the hospital and then at the rehab center," she said. "Now that I've started back to work part-time—I work at a doctor's office—I've been keeping Emma with me about half the time."

"Things might get better after the transition."

"I don't know." She glanced down at her wringing hands and lay them in her lap. "My parents are worried that I'm not up to the job of being Emma's guardian."

She didn't expect a guy she'd just met to come to her defense, but his silence made her wonder if he agreed with her parents.

"Sounds like you're up against a lot."

Lindsay told herself that those were just more well-meaning words, like so many she'd heard the last six months, but Joe's comment was so well-timed that it almost helped. Suddenly, she was reminded of another time that he'd helped, probably more than he realized.

"Thank you for giving me the poem at the hospital." His strange expression made her pause. "You are 'Joe' from 'to Joe' written at the top, aren't you?"

A guilty smile pulled at his lips. Instead of answering, he turned to watch two boys climbing a curly slide. Maybe it was good that she hadn't mentioned how her nurses had told her about the young police officer who spent several hours with her at the hospital.

Finally, Joe turned back to her. "It was an impulse. The poem, I mean. My friend, Cindy, gave it to me a long time ago. I don't know why I gave it to you." He shrugged. "I thought it might help."

"You were right. It did."

That Joe seemed surprised only puzzled Lindsay. If he hadn't really believed it would help, then why had he given it to her?

"You know how it says, 'Don't be afraid. You are a child of God. You are precious—'"

"I know what it says."

His short remark surprised her even more, so she watched him for several seconds and then tried again.

"I mean the poem really reminded me to trust in God. I was devastated after the accident. After everything. During those first, dark weeks, I really needed to be reminded to rely on Him."

She shook her head, breathing out a slow sigh. "Without my faith, I wouldn't have survived. You know, like in the beginning of Psalm 46, 'God is our refuge and strength, a very present help in trouble.'"

For a long time, Joe stared at her as if she'd just announced that the Earth was an asteroid or something. What was wrong with him? Was she not supposed to bring up the poem? Hadn't he expected her to figure out that he'd been the one to give it to her? Why was he so uncomfortable about it? She'd thought about telling him that she'd been carrying the poem in her purse for months, but she thought it would bother him even more.

Then he shook his head. "I don't get it."

"Get what?"

"How, after everything you've been through, can you possibly still believe?"

Chapter Three

How could I not?

Lindsay's words rang in Joe's ears as he carried her blanket to the car. He could think of a dozen reasons why anyone who'd been through all she'd been through wouldn't believe in God, and *she* couldn't think of any? One would be the preschooler Lindsay was pulling toward the parking lot as she struggled along with her cane.

Yet, with all that had happened, Lindsay Collins still believed. She even quoted scriptures, when the words had lost impact on him a long time ago. He couldn't understand her resilient faith. If a loving God existed, wouldn't Emma still have a mother? Wouldn't Joe still have his? Wouldn't his little-boy prayers have had an impact, instead of slamming against the ceiling while his mother wasted away in slow, deadly steps? And he wouldn't let himself get started on natural tragedies, like Hurricane Katrina, or manmade ones, like 9-11. Those wouldn't have happened, either, would they?

"I don't want to go to your house, Aunt Lindsay," Emma whined as they struggled along. "I want to go to *my* house."

"Sweetheart, that's not—" Lindsay stopped herself with a frustrated sigh.

Joe didn't have to wonder if her next word would have been "possible." Lindsay had already told him that Delia Banks's house had been sold as part of the estate. Emma would have a tough time understanding that she could never go home again.

"I want to go to my house," Emma hollered this time.

"Come on, Emma. We're leaving now."

Joe wanted to tell Lindsay she was handling the situation all wrong, but he doubted she would appreciate his opinion. Not for the first time this afternoon, he wondered if Brian and Donna Collins were right in questioning their daughter's ability to raise a child.

Maybe he should give her a few tips—no. He put a quick stop on the path his thoughts were taking. He'd already fulfilled his promise to tell her about the accident—well, most of it. He couldn't bring himself to tell her the rest. What possible good purpose would it have served? She already had some serious survivor's guilt. The last thing she needed was to learn that her pleas for help for her sister first had fallen on deaf ears. It was more likely that he just didn't want to confess that those deaf ears had been his.

"I don't want to go," Emma started again.

"You're just tired."

The little girl shook her head hard, her ponytails hitting her aunt's hip with each swing. "I'm not tired. I want to stay. Want to play with Trooper Joe."

He couldn't help but to smile at that, so he turned his head so they wouldn't see. Wasn't it just like a kid to forget what she was causing a ruckus about in the first place and to just keep arguing for the point of arguing?

She tried to pull Emma along again, but the child had gone limp. Lindsay couldn't pull her without falling.

"That's enough, Emma." Her jaw flexed as she gritted her teeth. "We have to get home, and Trooper Rossetti doesn't have time to play with us all afternoon."

"No!"

Emma jerked free from her aunt's hold, making Lindsay struggle to keep her balance. The little girl only made it a few steps toward the playground before Joe caught her around the waist and lifted her from the ground. He wasn't doing a good job of not getting further involved.

"Where are you going, Little Miss?"

"I want to play," she wailed.

Holding her away from him to avoid kicking legs, Joe started up the path toward the parking lot again. He had to give the child credit for her effort, but she'd picked an opponent accustomed to wrestling squirrelly suspects into handcuffs. It wasn't much of a contest.

"I'm sorry we can't play right now, but whipping around like a tornado isn't going to make anyone want to play with you."

After Emma settled in his arms as he'd hoped she would, he smiled at her. "Now, that's better."

Joe sensed before he saw Lindsay watching him. At his lifted brow, she mouthed the words "thank you," and then she struggled forward again. He hadn't done anything all that amazing, so it shouldn't have pleased him so much that he'd impressed her.

But as Lindsay stopped next to her car, Joe saw the reminder that it provided and felt the slap he deserved. The nondescript midsize with the child seat in the back was nothing like her sporty two-door that had fried in the accident. What was he thinking, trying to impress Lindsay Collins at all? Did he need any further reminders that he should cut his losses and put Lindsay and her niece in his rearview mirror without delay?

Lindsay opened the right-rear door and Joe handed the child to her.

"I want to play with Joe." Emma struggled against the constraints of Lindsay's arms.

The child's wiggling caused her aunt to lose her balance, the cane skidding from its position of support. On instinct, Joe reached out for them from behind, catching Lindsay and steadying her from beneath the elbows. He was almost convinced he felt her shiver under his touch. His fingers tingled so much from the contact that he almost opened his hands again and let the woman and child drop to the asphalt. What was wrong with him? That jolt inside him had to be the same adrenaline he felt at an accident scene. Any other type of reaction to Lindsay Collins would be unacceptable, and he wasn't about to cross *that* line.

As quickly as he could without being obvious in shoving her away, he set Lindsay back on her feet and released her. Ignoring the prickles in his fingers that refused to subside, he stepped up to Emma and tugged on one of her ponytails.

"Didn't we already talk about this tornado business?" He gave her a stern look. "We can make plans to play together again soon, but only if you stop this nonsense and let Aunt Lindsay buckle you in your seat."

Joe was as surprised as Lindsay appeared to be by his offer, but he guessed he shouldn't have been. He'd already been too personally involved in this case, and he'd chosen to dig in deeper the moment he'd suggested the trip to the park when he could have answered Lindsay's questions right in the Brighton Post parking lot.

But he'd had to make sure Lindsay and her niece would be okay, and now that he'd witnessed Lindsay's struggles, he couldn't resist stepping in to help. He was caught now in a trap of his own making. He should drive away as fast as the high-performance tires on his patrol car could carry him, but he knew he wouldn't, any more than he would leave a stranded motorist on the side of the interstate.

"Promise?"

Joe startled as Emma's question drew him back from his thoughts. Sitting docilely now in her aunt's arms, Emma looked back at him with a skeptical expression.

"That we can play together? Of course, I promise."

But Lindsay shook her head. "I don't think—"

"Come on. It will be fun."

Lindsay's jaw tightened as she buckled Emma in her seat and closed the car door. Finally, she turned back to him.

He held his hands up the way he usually expected suspects to do. "Before you say anything, let me make a suggestion. I really do have a lot of experience in taking care of kids, so maybe when we meet again I could give you some tips."

"You mean tips about how to *bribe* kids into behaving?"

Because her lips had formed a straight line, he couldn't help grinning at her. She had spunk. "Worked, didn't it? And it wasn't that big of a bribe anyway."

"You shouldn't have promised her."

"Why not?"

"Because you won't be able to keep that promise." She cleared her throat. "Look, I appreciate you taking the time to fill in the blanks for me about the accident, but now I have to put that night behind me so Emma and I can get on with our lives."

"You could make that life a little easier if you just let me—"

"Thank you. But no."

He used the lazy grin that usually swayed women to his side. "Okay, then. But remember, the offer still stands."

"Noted." She swallowed visibly, but showed no signs of caving. "Thanks again."

Lindsay hobbled around the car and climbed in as if she couldn't get away from him fast enough. She didn't look his way as she backed out of her parking place and started down the long drive to the park exit.

He knew he should just let her drive off into the southeast Michigan sunset, but he wouldn't. Whether she admitted it or not, Lindsay needed his help in figuring out how to handle Emma. He might not be able to do anything about the rest of her problems, might not be able to give Lindsay back her sister, or Emma her mother, but this was one area he could help if Lindsay would only let him.

Just like he didn't know her well enough to understand how her faith could have survived such a loss, she didn't know him, either. She had no idea how determined he could be, whether it was to get into the police academy or to keep a promise. And he was more determined than he'd been about anything in a long time to keep his promise to Emma and in turn help out the child's aunt. If he helped Lindsay adapt to her new life, then maybe, just maybe, he could escape from the weight of his guilt and get on with his own life.

"I'm so hungry." Emma put so much emphasis on "so" that it sounded more like she'd been starving for years rather than minutes.

"Be patient, sweetie. I'm not finished cooking yet." Lindsay had barely started, but it wouldn't help to tell Emma that. Lindsay had just changed from her work clothes into shorts and a T-shirt, and now she was banging around in the kitchen, hoping to finish before Emma had a meltdown.

"But I'm hungry *now*."

Lindsay glanced down to see that her hand that grasped the saucepan handle was trembling. She squeezed her eyes so tightly closed that her temples ached. Getting out of work late had caused her to be tardy in picking up Emma from the day-care center. Delia had never been late in the three years she'd taken Emma to that center. The director had made a point of telling Lindsay so. Worse than that, the woman had offered her words with a pitying smile.

This wasn't working. What made her think she could handle parenting? She didn't know what she was doing. She'd asked a three-year-old to be patient. Lindsay hadn't learned that skill, and she was well on her way to thirty.

"Lord, please give me patience." She whispered the prayer as she shoved the broiler pan in the oven.

Emma was sagging against the doorjamb, as if she were weak from starvation.

"Why don't you run into the living room and play with Monkey Man?"

"I don't want to play."

"Then maybe you could lay on the couch for a few minutes. Dinner will be ready real soon."

Emma looked doubtful, but slumped out of the room for what would only be a short reprieve. *Trooper Rossetti would have helped you out.* Lindsay shook off the thought. She might have been whining a few minutes before, but she didn't need help, least of all from Joe Rossetti.

Lindsay had resented every time images of the police officer crept into her thoughts at work today, so she'd spent most of the afternoon resenting. Why couldn't she get that man out of her mind? She had every reason to delete him from her mental hard drive, and yet he'd returned like an internet virus that refused to be wiped clean.

It couldn't be that she found the police officer unusually handsome and was replaying images of him for her own entertainment. Or that she'd enjoyed it so much when he steadied her at the park when she stumbled that she was daydreaming about repeating the clumsy move so he could come to her assistance again. No. Of course not.

The only reason she could be having any thoughts at all about Trooper Rossetti was that his answers yesterday had only caused her to have more questions. Like for instance, why he had spent so much time with her in the hospital after the accident. He hadn't said a word about it. And if Joe didn't believe in God, then why had he given her the poem that reminded her to have faith? If he'd given it to her on "impulse," as he'd said, then he must have once believed. Had there been some tragedy in his life that caused him to lose his faith?

"Stop it!"

She shot a glance over her shoulder, to see if Emma had returned to watch her again. But she was alone. She puffed up her cheeks and let the breath out slowly, hoping to expel her strange thoughts in the process. She had enough tragedy in her life, and too much on her plate right now, to be taking on someone else's problems.

Since no sounds were coming from the living room, except for the saccharine sound of Emma's favorite kids'-music CD, Lindsay was relieved that the child had found something with which to occupy herself for a few minutes. Now Lindsay would be able to finish making dinner in peace.

She lifted the pan lid and used a fork to test the doneness of the asparagus. She only needed to start on the salad and wait for the oven buzzer to go off for the salmon, and she would have a meal on the table. Maybe Emma would even like what she'd made for dinner this time.

But just as she chopped through a head of red cabbage, the doorbell rang.

"What now?"

She dropped the cabbage and knife on the cutting board and hurried down the hall to the living room.

"Remember, Emma, don't answer the—" The word "door" died on her lips as she glanced around the living room. Emma wasn't on the couch or near her pile of toys. Even her portable CD player lay abandoned.

"Emma?" Lindsay called, as she started up the stairs, her pulse scrambling. She expected the child to come racing down the hall. It and her bedroom were empty.

"Emma Claire, where are you?" She started down the steps again.

"Hey, Lindsay. Out here."

Her heart was pounding, but she stopped as she recognized the familiar voice coming from outside. What was Joe doing here? She hurried across the living room and opened the door. Joe stood on her porch with Emma resting on his hip. Lindsay could only stare at them, her mouth falling slack.

She wanted to yell at him for showing up at her condo after she'd expressly told him she didn't need his help, but how could she, when he was standing there holding the child she hadn't been watching closely enough? When Emma's escape was proof positive that she was doing a lousy job.

Joe stepped up to the storm door and opened it. "Look who just slipped out the front door to greet me."

"I can see that."

His smile grated on her. Okay, maybe she wasn't

the best guardian, but he didn't have to rub it in. He was the one who'd popped in uninvited and had given a three-year-old a reason to sneak outside. And if he was insisting on showing up as the protector of the public, why was he out of uniform again, wearing jeans and a snug T-shirt that hugged his well-formed arms, chest and shoulders? She didn't even want to think about whether she should have noticed those things at a time like this, or at any time for that matter.

"I was just telling Emma here that even when she sees a friend outside, she can't go out without her Aunt Lindsay." He lowered the child to the ground.

"Trooper Rossetti is right," Lindsay said, no matter how much it grated on her to admit it.

"Sorry," Emma said in a small voice.

"It's okay, but you'd better come inside now."

Lindsay made just enough room for her niece to slip past her, and then she reached for the door handle and tried to close it.

"Thanks for coming by, but it's a crazy time of day around here, and we were just about to eat, so…" She paused, hoping he would get the hint to leave, but the oven timer went off, and he still hadn't turned down the walk.

"Shouldn't you get that?"

"Yeah, I'd better."

She waved and started down the hall. She'd

only taken a few steps when a squeak of the door had her turning back. Emma had grabbed Joe's hand and was pulling him inside, and Joe was *letting* her. Was the trooper always this dense over social cues, or was he being this annoying on purpose?

"Do you want to play dolls?" Emma asked, as she led him toward the toy box Lindsay had moved from her old bedroom.

Lindsay started back toward them, but the buzz kept coming from the kitchen. Finally, with a frustrated sigh, she stalked out of the room.

Just as she pulled the pan from the oven, she sensed Joe behind her. Either that or the skin on the back of her neck was becoming gooseflesh for no good reason. Setting the pan aside, she turned to face him.

Joe stood in the doorway, with his thumbs hooked in his belt loops, like a blue-jeans model. Only his jeans had the spotted look of someone's painting pants, and the hole in one of the knees appeared to have been earned the hard way. At least he had the decency not to look smug that he'd managed to stay despite her wishes.

Lindsay peeked behind him, but Emma must have stayed in the living room.

"Wasn't I obvious enough that I was trying to get you to leave?"

The side of his mouth lifted. "No, you were real clear there."

"So why are you still here?"

"I was invited."

That lazy smile annoyed her, but the jolt of electricity she felt shocked her in more ways than one. What was wrong with her? She crossed her arms. Just who did he think he was, staying when he knew she didn't want him there? And an invitation from a three-year-old didn't count, either. Joe must have sensed that she was about to say something acidic enough to bore a hole through his skin because he held up both hands to ward off the assault.

"Look, I'm already here, so you might as well put me to work. I could hang out with Emma while you're finishing dinner. You said it's a hectic time of day, so…" He glanced around the chaos in her kitchen. "And, besides, Emma is already setting up dolls in the living room. Do you want to be the one to tell her I can't stay to play?"

Lindsay caught sight of her saucepan in her side vision. Steam was seeping from under the lid where the asparagus had to be overcooked. The head of cabbage lay on the cutting board where she'd abandoned it.

"Fine," she said, blowing out a frustrated sigh. "You can stay. But this is *my* house and *my* rules, and I—" She stopped, wincing. "Did I really just say that?"

"From your parents?"

"My dad."

"My brother tells me that, as a parent, you say every one of those things you promised yourself you'll never say to your own kids."

In a roundabout way, he'd just called her a parent. During all of the discussions with her mother and father and even with Delia's attorney, no one had called Lindsay a "parent." She liked the way that sounded.

"So…?" Joe gestured toward the living room with a flick of his thumb.

"Go ahead. Just play with Emma until I can get food on the table."

Farther down the hall, he turned back. "I'll be sure to follow *your* rules. In *your* house." With a grin, he was off and around the corner to the living room.

Emma must have been hiding because giggles drifted down the hall. Lindsay could tell the exact moment when Joe found her hiding place as those giggles multiplied. Joe really was amazing with her niece. Fun but firm. Playful but not a pushover. Maybe he could teach her a few things about working with children.

No matter what it took for her to become the best caregiver for Emma, the kind that Delia had hoped for when she'd named her guardian, Lindsay was willing to do it. And if that meant taking unsolicited advice from a Michigan State Trooper, then she would do that, too.

"You could stay for dinner," she heard herself saying.

Joe popped around the corner with Emma hanging on his leg. "Sure, I'd love to stay. Thanks."

Lindsay nodded. He'd won. She should have been frustrated that he'd gotten his way, after all. But she was relieved that Trooper Joe Rossetti *wasn't* leaving, and she couldn't explain why.

Yet, relief wasn't the worst of what she was feeling. Her sweaty palms and the butterflies in her belly felt an awful lot like anticipation. Was she really looking forward to sharing dinner with the guy who reminded her of everything she'd lost and whose presence there today was like a neon sign announcing her weaknesses as a guardian? Even telling herself that he was there on her terms, not his, didn't make her feel any less edgy. Anticipation…now, that worried her most of all.

Chapter Four

"That was great," Joe said, as he pushed back from Lindsay's blond-wood dinette table and wiped his mouth on a cloth napkin.

A pretty pink blush crept across Lindsay's cheeks, and she stared down at her plate. "No, it wasn't. The salmon was overdone, and the asparagus was as limp as pasta noodles."

"I happen to like pasta noodles, even when they're well past al dente." He also liked the little smile that spread on her lips over the compliment and how pretty she looked in her T-shirt, cutoffs and ponytail, but he kept those things to himself. No need to ruin a pleasant dinner by getting himself tossed out on his ear.

"Then you should have *loved* that stuff."

"It was fish." Emma's tone left little doubt about what she thought about fruits of the sea.

Joe and Lindsay looked at each other across

the table and laughed. They'd done an awful lot of laughing over this dinner, which had started out tense at best. Mostly, they'd laughed about the antics of the three-year-old who sat in a booster seat so high that her knees bumped the table edge. Occasionally, though, they'd found something funny that one of the adults had said, as well.

"I guess that says it all when you're three," Joe said when the laughter died down.

"I should have known better than to cook fish for a child, anyway," Lindsay said with a frown.

"Some kids like fish," he said because she seemed to need some kind words.

"I don't like it." Emma made another face.

"Not *that* one, apparently." Lindsay tilted her head to indicate the child who'd eaten only enough to survive, mostly pushing her food around on her plate to create little pink-and-green piles.

Not most of the kids he'd ever met, either, but Joe didn't mention that. And asparagus was seldom a hit with the under-ten crowd. He kept that to himself, as well.

After Lindsay sent Emma upstairs to get her pajamas ready for her bath, she started stacking the dishes. "Dinner's a daily battle around here."

Joe carried several plates to the counter. "Have you ever considered making 'kid-friendly' meals like pizza, chicken fingers and mac and cheese?"

He was glad she hadn't lifted her stack of serving dishes because as aghast as she looked, she would have dropped the whole thing on the floor.

"I don't want to feed her that stuff. What kind of guardian would I—"

She stopped herself, but he got the gist of what she was saying. "Plenty of people give their children kid food. Do you think they're all bad parents?"

"Of course not, but I…" She let her words trail away and shrugged.

"You're awfully hard on yourself, aren't you? My brother and I survived for a whole year on grilled cheese sandwiches and tomato soup after—well, we survived, anyway."

Lindsay turned back from the dishwasher with curiosity in her eyes. "Why did you—"

"Never mind. It's not that interesting a story." He was sorry he'd mentioned it. Since when did he talk about his mother's death and the lost years that had followed it? Rather than stand back and give Lindsay the chance to ask more questions, he helped her load the dishwasher.

"All I'm saying is, you should relax and give yourself a break. It's okay for kids to have those things sometimes. It's all about balance."

He thought he'd been convincing, but Lindsay only started shaking her head.

"I have to get this right. To be the best guardian for Emma. I have to do it for her…and for Delia."

Immediately, her eyes filled, but Lindsay blinked back her tears. "I *will* get it right."

"And I thought you were just worried about some deep-fried balls of processed chicken and globs of high-fat cheese mixed in with carbohydrate-filled pasta noodles."

It wasn't the best timing for a joke, but Joe either had to tell one or allow the emotion clogging his throat to really embarrass him. This all hit a little too close to home, to two little boys and the father who'd been forced to raise them alone.

"I was worried about those things, too."

He couldn't decide whether it was her smile or her determination that dazzled him, but he heard himself saying, "You'll get it right. I know it."

Lindsay stared back at him with wide eyes. Why did she find his statement of belief in her so surprising? He'd already said too much, yet he was tempted to say more, to tell her how impressed he was by her determination and her loyalty. That he'd thought those qualities were exclusive to people in uniform, not pretty redheads with the cutest freckles on their noses.

Okay, he wouldn't have said that, but still he was grateful when the sound of a faucet from upstairs made sure he wouldn't have the chance. A literal gift from above.

"Uh-oh." Lindsay glanced up to the ceiling before starting for the stairs. "Emma, honey, please turn off the water until I get there."

She seemed surprised when the faucet squeaked off again, as if she hadn't expected the child to obey her.

"Well, I'd better get up there before she goes tub diving." She started out of the kitchen, but then stopped and turned back to him. "Do you want to—"

"See myself out? Sure." He hoped he didn't sound as disappointed as he felt.

She blushed just like she had when he'd complimented her cooking. "Uh...I was going to ask if you wanted to wait here until I finish with Emma's bath and her bedtime story, but if you need to get home—"

"I could stay," he rushed to say. Yes, he could, but the question was whether he *should*. His sweaty hands and dry mouth suggested that answer was a big "no."

"I'll finish cleaning up the kitchen while you're doing that."

"You don't have to."

He waved off her refusal. "It will keep me occupied while I wait."

"Okay, then."

She appeared as nervous as she had two days before, when she'd shown up at the Brighton Post to dig around in a recent past that would have been better left undisturbed. He listened for her footfalls on the steps, and then the sound of running water upstairs, before collecting the pans on the stove and filling the sink to wash them.

But all he could think about as he scrubbed the pans and wiped down the counters was what he was still doing in Lindsay Collins's condo when the child he was concerned about wouldn't be around for the rest of the night. He was still helping out, right? He was here because he wanted to come to Lindsay's aid to relieve his guilt over the accident and what he'd failed to tell her about it. Only those things.

"Yeah, you keep telling yourself that, buddy," he said under his breath.

"Did you say something?"

Caught, Joe shut off the faucet and turned to face her. The running water, as he rinsed down the sink, must have been what kept him from noticing her approach. His senses were off with her. Until lately, he wouldn't even have considered it possible that someone would be able to sneak up on him, and she'd done it without even trying.

Lindsay stood in the doorway with her arms crossed, her frustration obvious in the hard set of her jaw.

"It was nothing." He cocked his head to the side. "Boy, that was a quick bath and story. What was it, a picture book?"

But Lindsay didn't smile the way he'd hoped she would. If anything, her posture tightened.

"No book at all. Just a bath."

"Oh, weren't you planning to read—"

"I was. We read a book together every night. It's one thing that she used to do with Delia that I've tried to continue every night she's with me. It keeps away her nightmares. Usually."

"Don't feel as if you need to change your night-time schedule just because I'm here." That was all he needed, for his presence there to make things worse between Lindsay and her niece. "In fact, you really shouldn't change—"

"I didn't."

Joe stared at her. She wasn't making sense. The same woman who was afraid to let her niece munch on a few chicken nuggets was just going to blow off one of their few daily routines because they had company.

"I don't understand."

"She didn't want me to read a story to her to-night." She blew out a frustrated breath. "She wants you."

Lindsay expected gloating when Joe joined her on the tiny deck a half hour later, after story time with Emma. Time that should have been hers. How would she prove to her parents, a judge in the custody proceeding and even herself that she was the right guardian for Emma if she couldn't even get the child to choose her as the person to read her a bedtime story?

This was what she deserved for inviting Joe to stay just because she needed adult conversation. Okay, who was she kidding? She'd invited him to stay because he was easy on the eyes, and he'd made her laugh all night. No matter how flattering the attention he paid her was, Lindsay needed to remember he was only there for Emma.

Shifting in one of the chairs in her faux wicker deck set so she could straighten her stiff leg, Lindsay watched him and waited.

But Joe didn't say anything at all as he stood resting his hands on the rail and staring out into the wooded area at the back of her complex.

"Well, did she go to sleep?" she asked finally.

"She was about to when I left," he answered without looking back at her. "She asked me to leave the closet light on."

"She likes that. Can I get you some iced tea?"

"Maybe in a while."

She waited for him to tell her more, but he seemed strangely subdued as he continued to look out into the darkness. "What book did she choose for you to read?"

"Love You Forever."

"The one by Robert Munsch?" Now she understood why he'd become so quiet. She could barely avoid choking up when she read Emma that story about a lullaby that a mother sang to her son. "She picks that book a lot. Delia used to sing parts of it to her."

"She told me."

His eyes were shiny when he turned back to her, but it might have been just from the fancy streetlights that lit the walking path through the woods. She'd been ready to be angry with him because Emma had chosen him over her, but it was hard to hold a grudge against someone so obviously moved by the story.

"Don't tell me you sang it to her, too, or I'm going to give up right now and crawl into a hole."

He smiled at that. "Oh, no. I wouldn't do that. No kid deserves that kind of punishment."

"You mean you're not good at everything?"

"Not by a long shot. Do you sing it to her when you read it?"

"Oh, no. I happen to like my niece."

"Funny." Appearing more relaxed than he had been since coming outside, he backed away from the rail and settled into the second chair, with a tiny table between them.

She stared out into the same night that Joe had been watching with faraway thoughts a few minutes before. "Delia had an amazing singing voice."

His only answer was a nod.

"That was just one of the things she was good

at." She couldn't help smiling at the memory of the sister she adored. "Everybody loved her. She was smart and beautiful and generous. Voted both Homecoming Queen and 'Most Likely to Succeed.' She was amazing."

"Sounds like it."

"She was a doctor, you know."

"Your parents mentioned it."

There was a flash of something unreadable in his eyes, but he didn't say more.

"She could have gone into any specialty, but she chose family practice because she thought she could help the most people that way." Lindsay smiled again. "Did you know she was still in her residency when her husband died? Complications from diabetes. She still managed to finish the program and join a group practice, all while still being a great mom to Emma."

"She sounds amazing."

"She was."

"Didn't you say you also worked in the medical field?"

The surprise on Lindsay's face over his question bothered Joe. Was she shocked that he remembered that she'd mentioned her work, or that he was more interested in knowing about her than her late sister?

"I'm an ultrasound technician."

When she didn't say more, he asked, "You said you worked in a doctor's office?"

"A women's practice." She repositioned herself as though her leg was becoming stiff again. "Most of my ultrasounds are on OB patients."

"It sounds like fun work."

"Sometimes."

Joe waited and kept waiting. Okay, he could imagine times when her work would be difficult—when the test showed abnormalities or worse—but still, he would have expected her to tell him how much she enjoyed introducing parents to their babies for the first time. To at least tell him a little more.

"So…how long have you worked as a state trooper?"

She was watching him when he looked over at her. He answered her questions—ten years on the force, a commendation on his record—but it bothered him that she'd changed the subject.

Why was Lindsay more comfortable talking about Delia's accomplishments than her own? Had someone led her to believe that her achievements were less valuable than her sister's, or was it just survivor's guilt that made Lindsay gush about Delia? He'd already gotten the sense that Lindsay had no idea how beautiful she was, but was there more to it? Did she see herself as second-class?

"Was your sister a runner like you?"

Again, she looked surprised, as if he'd discovered a long-buried secret or something. "I saw all those certificates and medals in the hall."

"Oh. Right. I used to run 5Ks. But Delia? Oh, no. She said, for her to run three-point-one miles, there'd better be a mall at the finish line."

She was grinning as she said it, so he grinned back, pleased that he'd found something she'd done better than her sister. It was unkind to think like this about someone who'd passed away, but Joe could only imagine how hard it had been for Lindsay to compete against an overachieving sibling who was even more revered in death.

"Are you a runner, too?" She cleared her throat. "I mean, are you a runner?"

He didn't miss that she'd just excluded herself from the group. "Me? A runner? No way. I'd rather have all of my fingernails pulled off with pliers."

"Pliers?"

"Maybe nothing that violent, but you get the picture."

"But you do something. It's obvious you work out."

"Is it?"

Her only answer was a crimson flush that spread even to her ears. It was hardly a new thing for Joe to have women noticing him. He didn't miss the furtive looks, but he rarely thought twice about them. So why was he impressed that Lindsay had all but admitted she'd been looking? She had to be the first woman who seemed so humiliated that *he knew* she'd been looking, though, so he let her off the hook.

"I just do weight training mostly. And the stair climber for cardio."

"It's healthy to do something."

"From all those awards, I'm guessing you're a pretty good runner. Your parents have to be so proud." The last he added on impulse, based on an instinct he used to be able to trust before and hoped he still could.

"That's in the past. It was just a hobby, anyway."

When he glanced at her, she was staring at the deck boards beneath her bare feet rather than at him. She'd said running was in her past. Probably six months and one pelvis fracture ago. Another thing she'd lost with the accident. She'd called running a hobby when her wall of certificates suggested a passion. She hadn't even answered his question about her parents, and he could guess why. He suspected that all had not been well with the Collins family long before the accident.

"Well, it's getting late," she said.

Joe glanced down at his watch, sorry he'd brought up the certificates. It was only 8:45 p.m., a good curfew for sixth-graders. "So it is."

For someone who'd invited him to stay after

dinner, she was suddenly in a hurry for him to leave. So much for the iced tea. Well, she'd allowed him to stay for dinner when she would have preferred for him to go, so he could be gracious now.

"Yeah, I should be getting home. Work's going to come awfully early tomorrow."

She didn't argue, but stood and opened the slider so she could lead him through to the front door. He followed, matching her slower pace. When she reached the door, she turned back to him and straightened her shoulders.

"I appreciate your coming here, even though I didn't exactly encourage it. Come to think of it, I emphatically discouraged it, but thank you anyway…for Emma's sake. I'm even thanking you for the tips."

"You're welcome, I think." He'd been looking for an opportunity, so he pulled a card from his wallet. With a pen from the end table, he wrote on it and held it out to her. "Here. That's my personal cell on the back. Call me. I mean…you know…if you have any problems with Emma."

Lindsay shook her head and stared at his hand until he lowered it.

"Look, I understand that you're concerned about Emma, but you don't need to be. Thank you again, but we won't be needing any further help." She nodded as if to emphasize her point. "Emma and I will be just fine on our own. I'll make sure of it."

"I'm glad to hear that." Still, he couldn't help but lift his hand and extend the card again. "Here, take this anyway. Just in case."

Joe couldn't explain it. He wasn't suggesting that Lindsay couldn't make it on her own, but it had become important to him that he left something of himself behind with her. Whether or not she called, he liked knowing she could. After tonight, he would have no reason to ever see her again. No legitimate reason. He could keep coming up with excuses as he had tonight, but stalking was a misdemeanor in Michigan. Even a felony with aggravated circumstances. Hadn't he aggravated her enough already?

She stared at the card for a long time, but finally she reached out to take it. He didn't miss that she was careful not to let their fingers brush. That was probably a good idea. He'd already experienced the electric shock of touching Lindsay Collins. It wouldn't be in his best interest to repeat that.

"Thanks, but I won't need it." Instead of holding on to the card, she set it on the table next to the pen. She pulled open the front door and then pushed the storm door wide and looked back at him.

Stepping through the doorway, he couldn't resist one more look back at her. "Thanks for dinner."

After they said their goodbyes, she pulled the storm door closed, shut the door behind it and clicked two locks. Joe stood there, feeling discarded in a way he couldn't remember ever having been before. Finally, he started down the walk to his truck. But disconcerting thoughts slipped inside the cab with him, buckling themselves in the passenger seat and refusing to budge.

What was it about Lindsay Collins that made it so hard for him to get her out of his mind? She was facing so many challenges. Even parents who didn't appear to be in her corner. But he'd never seen anyone as determined do to anything as Lindsay was to be a good guardian.

She probably wouldn't get everything right the first time, but she wouldn't stop trying. The child victims in the tragic domestic-assault cases he'd investigated would have given anything to have someone try that hard for them.

It was probably best that he wouldn't see Lindsay after today. If he did spend time with her, he would only be tempted to become friends with her. Or worse. That just couldn't happen. He couldn't allow himself to become too involved. Letting his guard down had gotten him into trouble both in his personal life and on the job. Shouldn't he learn from his mistakes?

Just because he wouldn't be spending more time with her didn't mean he didn't want her to succeed, though. He might not get the chance to watch her as she took each step along the learning curve to become the best guardian she could be, but, at least in his thoughts, he would be rooting for her every step of the way.

Chapter Five

With trembling hands, Lindsay dug her cell phone out of her purse and fumbled with the buttons. She didn't want to dial the number—it felt like admitting defeat—but this was what she had to do.

It didn't matter that it was nearly 2:00 a.m. or that just over twenty-four hours earlier she'd said she didn't need the number. But this wasn't about her. It was about Emma, and Lindsay would do anything to ensure that the child was okay. Well, except call her parents. Anything but that. But she could do this for her niece, and she would swallow her pride with barely a sour taste to do it.

She cast another worried glance at the top of the stairs where Emma stood, continuing to sob.

Lindsay had tried. In the more than an hour since Emma had awakened from a nightmare screaming, Lindsay had held her, brushed back her hair and rubbed her back. But nothing she did comforted Emma even a little. The child had just continued wailing and asking for her mommy.

The one thing Lindsay couldn't give her.

Sometimes she even cried for Trooper Joe.

Lindsay had prayed often during this time, too, but Emma had just kept on crying. But then Lindsay had remembered her minister's words about part of praying being listening for God's call to act. She had to act now. She might not be able to give Emma her mommy, but she could fulfill her second request.

Emma couldn't keep going like this or she would make herself sick. And then there were the neighbors to worry about, people living only a wall away in their attached condos. Would someone call the police because they were disturbing the peace?

Because she hadn't entered the number in her contacts, she read it from the card and dialed. He answered on the second ring.

"Rossetti."

"Joe? I mean…Trooper Joe…ah, Trooper Rossetti?"

"Lindsay? Is that you? Is everything all right? Just relax and tell me."

She would have thought that he'd just recognized her number from his cell's caller ID, but she hadn't given him *her* number. Still, he'd known her voice, even probably coming out of a REM sleep cycle. Immediately, a rush of calm flooded through Lindsay, although she couldn't decide whether it was his words or his soothing voice. She cleared her throat, but he didn't give her a chance to talk.

"Lindsay? Lindsay?" His voice was louder this time, not calm at all. "What is that sound?"

She glanced over her shoulder to find that Emma had scooted farther down on the stairs and was sitting on a step, looking pitiful and small as she continued crying.

"It's Emma," she called out, trying to talk over the noise. "She had a nightmare, and she's hysterical. Nothing I do seems to help." She cleared her throat and then shoved right through her pride. "Would you be willing—"

"I'll be there in ten."

He clicked off the call before she could say thank you. Or change her mind. She wouldn't allow herself to second-guess anyway. Joe was coming. She didn't care if forty-eight hours ago she had insisted she didn't need any help from anyone, Joe least of all. Now she was just relieved he was willing to help.

Unlocking the door, Lindsay climbed halfway up the staircase and sat on a step, using the rail to steady herself in the absence of her cane. Still sobbing, Emma scrambled into her lap and curled into a little-girl ball.

"It's going to be okay, sweetie," she whispered, as she brushed back Emma's sweaty hair, so soft and dark like her mother's. "*We're* going to be okay."

From her perch on the staircase, Lindsay rocked the precious cargo in her arms, the edge of the step biting into her back every time she rocked backward. She didn't know any lullabies, so she hummed "The Old Rugged Cross" instead. Closing her eyes, she let the song be a prayer.

Lindsay didn't know how much time had passed before she heard a quiet knock on her front door and then the turn of the unlocked doorknob. It took her a second to realize that she'd heard both of those sounds because Emma was no longer making any noise. The child curled against her was asleep. Lindsay couldn't believe her eyes.

Joe stuck his head inside the door and looked around the room. "Lindsay?"

"Up here," she answered, just above a whisper.

He glanced up, his gaze stopping on the two of them. "So everything's okay?"

She lifted a shoulder and lowered it, causing Emma to shift on her lap. "False alarm, I guess."

"Probably just tripped it a little prematurely."

"Maybe."

Joe closed the door behind him. "Interesting place for rocking."

"Whatever it takes."

He nodded as if he understood that ignoring her pride and calling him was whatever it took that night.

"Do you want me to help you get her to bed?"

Lindsay moved her leg and winced. "I'm so stiff that I might need some help up."

"Let's see what we can do."

We. She liked the sound of that. It didn't make her feel so alone. She allowed him to lift Emma, and then she tightened the belt on her bathrobe over her pajamas and settled back to wait. He would get to her after he put Emma back in her bed.

"You're going to have to help me out here," he said. "I won't have enough hands if you don't reach up to me."

"Oh. Right."

As she raised a hand to him, he shifted Emma's weight to one side, so he could pull Lindsay to her feet with the other hand. She ignored the tingle on her skin where their hands had connected. Why did she feel that way every time he touched her?

"Are you going to be okay?"

"I've got it from here." She clasped the rail, wincing at the dull ache in her hip.

"Are you sure you're all right?"

"I'm fine."

Appearing skeptical, he started up the stairs, and she followed behind him. In Emma's room, he lowered the child on the bright pink sheets she'd torn apart during her nightmare. Lindsay straightened the bedding and tucked the top sheet under Emma's chin. She kissed that mass of dark hair and started for the door, but when she turned back Joe was dropping a kiss on the child's head as well. The moment was so touching that a knot of emotion formed in her throat.

"I'm sorry for calling," Lindsay said, after they'd stepped outside the room and closed the door behind them.

"Why would you be sorry?"

She let him go down the stairs first and then gripped the rail and followed him in a slow, step-together-step pattern. "Because I called you in the middle of the night, woke you up and made you come here, and then I didn't even really need any help."

"Did you think you needed it when you called?"

"Well, sure, but—"

"Then I'm glad you trusted me enough to call." He turned back to her when he reached the landing. "I wasn't asleep when you called, anyway."

She lifted a brow. "A fan of late-night infomercials?"

"Insomnia. It's a recent condition."

"Well, the least I can do after you came to my

rescue is to offer you a cup of chamomile to help you sleep when you get back home." She led the way into the kitchen.

"I won't go back to bed," he said, but he still followed her. "I have to be to the post by oh-six-hundred hours."

"Sorry. Really."

"Don't worry about it. I wouldn't have come if I didn't want to." He tilted his head to the side and studied her. "What about you? Sure you wouldn't rather send me out so at least one of us can catch some shut-eye?"

"I won't be able to sleep now, either. Neither will any of my neighbors."

She put the kettle on the stove and pulled two mugs and the box of chamomile tea from the cabinet. After Lindsay placed a bag in each mug, Joe carried them to the table.

"So, should we invite them over for tea, too?"

She shook her head. "I wouldn't earn a 'Neighbor-of-the-Month Award' this morning. I'm feeling blessed that I'm a homeowner rather than a renter. Otherwise, Emma and I would be out on the street."

"Come on, Lindsay. Kids cry in every neighborhood. Some even have nightmares. It's annoying, and a few people might consider aggravated assault over it. But eviction? Oh, no. That's too extreme."

Joe had hoped Lindsay would laugh at his joke, but she only looked back at him with a stark expression.

"You should have heard her screaming. It was horrible. She was crying for her mommy. I didn't have any way to comfort her."

"You were doing a good job when I got here. She was sleeping like a baby."

That fact had shocked him and disappointed him more than he cared to admit. Had Lindsay needed his help with her niece so badly, or had he only wanted her to need him? Evidence wasn't in his favor, especially when it had taken him only thirty seconds to throw over the promise he'd made to himself to back out of Lindsay's life.

He hadn't even taken the time to wonder whether rushing to her rescue might hinder rather than help her to get on her own two feet. Didn't he want to ensure that the victim became self-sufficient, so he could put that accident behind him and restore his confidence on the job?

When the teakettle whistled, Lindsay carried it to the table and poured. "Emma just cried herself out and was exhausted. I only happened to be there when it happened."

Joe knew he shouldn't speak up, but he couldn't stop himself. "You don't give yourself enough credit. You were *with* her. In fact, you've been there for Emma as much as you possibly could since you got out of the hospital."

"What if it isn't enough?"

Her whispered words tore at his heart. He knew what it felt like to wonder if his best wasn't good enough. He understood the helplessness and regret intimately. Never would he wish that uncertainty on anyone.

"It has to be enough," he said. "You're all she has."

"Except my parents." Instead of adding more, Lindsay sat staring at her hands that encircled her coffee mug.

"Why didn't you call your parents when you couldn't get Emma to stop crying?"

"I couldn't." She shook her head hard, as though she couldn't fathom the thought. "They already think I'm not the best guardian for Emma. If I called them in a panic, it would only prove them—"

"Right," they said at the same time, his word a question, hers a statement.

She looked so miserable that Joe was tempted to reach out and take the hand that still cradled her mug. Why did some unwelcome protective side of him rise up right then, like a mother grizzly standing on hind legs to protect her cubs? Come to think of it, why weren't Lindsay's parents rising up to support her, rather than questioning her?

"So you called me instead—as the less horrifying of the two choices?"

"No, it wasn't like—" She stopped herself and frowned as she must have realized he was joking. "Funny."

"I have my moments."

"And she did sort of ask for you, too."

"Oh, sorry."

"Anyway, I had to call someone," she explained. "All of my church friends are also my parents' friends, and they might get worried and tell Mom and Dad. And my work friends…well, they're all busy and already sacrificing so I can work part-time, and…"

"And I did offer."

"Yes, you offered."

"So that means we're friends now?"

She smiled this time. "Guess so."

He couldn't help being pleased that she'd reached out to him, even if she'd considered all other choices first. He liked that she thought of him as a friend, too. She didn't seem to have many of those, at least not many real ones whose loyalty was to her alone. He might not have been able to tell her the whole story about the accident, but she'd asked for his support, and he could give that.

"Why don't your parents think you'll be a good guardian?"

"You've seen me with Emma." She shrugged. "I'm not exactly a natural with kids."

"A lot of people don't have strong natural instincts for working with kids. They still do just fine as parents. Like in everything else, determination and effort are more important than natural ability."

"I sure hope so."

Joe had seen Lindsay with Emma, all right, trying so hard when the child was tired and frustrated. He'd watched her tonight, too, rocking her little niece from her uncomfortable seat on the stairs, with fear and worry etched on her face. The image had nearly dropped him to his knees when he'd stood watching her in the doorway, and even now the memory of it touched a place inside him that had been clearly marked "No Trespassing" for a long time.

But he couldn't tell Lindsay that. He was the kind of guy who took down armed suspects and then stopped for a hearty breakfast, not the kind of guy who became choked up watching a woman cradling a sleeping child.

"Anyway, I can't be upset with my parents about this."

Her words drew him back from his strange thoughts.

"Why not?"

"Mom and Dad just have Emma's best interest

at heart. With Delia gone, they can't help wanting to protect their granddaughter."

"From their own daughter?"

"It's not like that," she insisted.

"Then what is it like with you and your family?"

"It's just that it's tough following behind a sibling who was so good at everything."

"Oh, good," he said. "I was beginning to think you were incapable of jealousy."

"What? Oh, I wasn't jealous. Not really." But then a smile spread on her lips. "Okay, maybe I felt a little invisible around her sometimes. Could she help it if she was amazing? If she deserved to shine?"

No wonder Lindsay had wanted to know why he'd saved her first instead of her sister. That Delia was needed more because she had a child was only part of it. Long before the night of the accident, someone had convinced her that her sister was more valuable than she was. After realizing this, how could he tell her the rest of the story about the night of the accident, about her pleas on the sister's behalf?

"Did your parents make you feel invisible?"

"No. Or at least if they did, they would never have intended to. They just wanted me to be more like her. To be more dedicated. More determined to succeed." She held her hands wide. "None of those were bad things. How could I blame them for wanting me to be more like her?"

Maybe she couldn't blame them, but he could. What kind of parents so obviously favored one of their children over the other one, no matter how awesome she was? And what kind of parent could fail to see how amazing Lindsay was? But he didn't tell her any of that. How could he without admitting that he'd been thinking about her too much himself?

"I know something about high expectations," he said instead.

"How's that?"

"I'm a third-generation Michigan State Trooper, and my grandfather and father were Gino and Leo Rossetti, two of the most decorated post commanders in Michigan history. Do you think there are any expectations in that?"

"Some," she said with a smile.

"For Christmas every year, Dad got my brother and me new police badges, holsters and model police cars. Joey Rossetti never would have been caught dead playing cowboys and outlaws. David and I were hard-nosed police detectives, and we were always chasing fleeing suspects."

"Joey?"

"Old nickname," he explained. "I outgrew that one a few decades ago, so it's off-limits."

"I'll keep that in mind." Sipping her tea, she set the cup back on the table. "You do understand."

He lifted a brow, waiting for her to explain.

"The expectations."

"I understand, all right."

"So, is your brother a trooper, too?"

"Surprisingly, no. There was practically a national incident when David decided not to join the 'family business,' but Dad and Grandpa eventually got over it. David didn't escape the whole law-enforcement bug completely, though. He and his wife are both assistant prosecutors in Kalamazoo."

"Then let me guess. Your mom's a judge."

His game face must have faltered a bit because her gaze narrowed. "Oh, no. You haven't mentioned your mom at all. She's not—"

He nodded. "She died when I was eight and David was twelve. Cancer."

"I'm sorry. I didn't know."

"You couldn't have known. Don't worry about it."

Strange how he was tempted to tell Lindsay more about his mother. He never talked about her. But for some reason, he wanted Lindsay to know that it was his mother's death, rather than his father's life, that led him to a career in law enforcement. He wanted to tell her other things, too, as if Lindsay's accident bound them somehow, making him want her to know as much about him as he knew about her.

It was a bad idea for him to allow himself to get too close to Lindsay and Emma. He didn't do that with people. He'd tried that once with Chelsea, but that relationship had gone up in flames as a reminder that his walls were there for a good reason. Lindsay was wearing down his defenses now, and he was letting it happen.

"I'm sorry I bought it up."

Joe blinked, realizing that she'd guessed he was still thinking about his mother.

"No. It's fine, really. I was just thinking about work." As far as *work* involved a certain victim in one of his accident cases, anyway.

She nodded, accepting his flimsy explanation.

"It's going to be really hot again tomorrow," she began. "I was thinking that…maybe…since I don't work tomorrow…that Emma and I would go to the beach at Kensington Metropark." She cleared her throat. "Would you like to meet us there?"

"The beach?"

Joe was grateful that at least his voice hadn't cracked. This was different from yesterday, when he'd invited himself to her condo to give her unsolicited advice, or even an hour ago, when she'd called him out of desperation. She'd invited *him*.

"You know, the place with the water and the sand?"

"Oh, I meant *which* beach at Kensington. You know there are two at that park, right?" And good thing for him that there were because he hadn't been this awkward around a female since the eighth grade.

"Martindale Beach, I guess. If you'll be too tired after tonight and after your shift tomorrow, I'll under—"

"Sounds like fun," Joe answered before she could offer to understand anything. She'd spent too much time *understanding*. From parents who didn't deserve any excuses to a sister who probably hadn't tried hard enough to share the stage. Even from a guy like him, who didn't have the guts to tell her the whole truth.

"Are you sure? It's just that I wanted to take Emma, and I'm worried that I might need an extra pair of hands."

"I'd be happy to go."

"Oh. Thanks."

Lindsay needed him, after all, as a friend. She deserved to have someone on her side for once, at least until she became confident enough to challenge her parents' belief that she wouldn't make a good guardian. He shouldn't get closer to her.

It was a risk, and he had enough of those at work with him clearly being off his game. But there was no way that he would leave this condo without letting Lindsay know one thing: she was not alone.

Chapter Six

Joe threw his police cruiser into Park and slammed his laptop next to him with such force that he had to open it again to see if he'd caused any damage. He would have a tough time explaining to Lieutenant Dawson that he'd destroyed state property all because he was frustrated.

He shook his head as he shoved open the car door. *Frustrated* didn't begin to describe what he'd been feeling from the moment he'd pulled his patrol car out on Interstate 96 this morning. Okay, he was exhausted from operating on less sleep than even the minuscule amount that had been his norm since a certain redhead had shown up and sent his focus careening off course. Still, even that didn't account for the sense of foreboding that had settled like a concrete block on his chest.

"Well, look what the cat dragged in."

Joe jerked at the sound and turned to give Trooper Celeste Addington a look that could kill. But Celeste and Trooper Brody Davison were standing less than ten feet away from him, and both were grinning like they knew a secret. His secret. How could he have missed their approach, if not in his side-view mirror, then at least from the thuds of their boots? Were his nerves wound so tightly that his hearing was on the blink, too?

"Both of you will give me some space today, if you know what's good for you."

He tilted his head, trying to stretch his neck, but he doubted even a masseuse could get the kinks out after an eight-hour shift with his muscles in a constant state of flex.

Brody, one of the new academy graduates to be assigned to the Brighton Post, bent his massive frame and leaned his head toward the petite brunette. "He's telling us to back off. I think that's downright unfriendly."

"Yeah. The cat that dragged him probably wishes she'd left him outside." Celeste removed her hat and brushed at the few hairs that had escaped from her tight bun.

Straightening, Brody looked over to Joe again. "I sure hope you weren't using that nice-guy treatment when you were dealing with the public today."

"Just part of my charm."

"Yeah, you're charming the way Oscar the Grouch is charming," Celeste said. "Especially the last few days."

Joe frowned. So much for nobody noticing that his head was out of the game. "I don't know about you two, but I've got work to do."

He brushed past them and headed to the building's back entrance. That laughter followed him all the way inside and only unsettled him more. Usually, he would have been telling the jokes, but there was no "usual" for him since the accident had messed with his confidence.

He'd just slumped into one of the open office chairs and logged on to the desktop computer when he had the prickly sense that he wasn't alone. He glanced back over his shoulder to find his best friend, Brett Lancaster, watching him.

"What are you looking at, Lancaster? I mean Lieutenant, sir." He stood up from his seat. For some reason, he just couldn't remember to call his former partner by his new job title.

Brett crossed his arms. "Chill out, Rossetti."

The two stood in a staring standoff until Brett spoke up again. "I hear you were in rare form all morning. All week, if we're being honest here."

"I was unaware my bad moods made headlines."

"They do, when even Clara comments on it."

It was Joe's turn to cross his arms. "List a few things that Clara Morrison hasn't made a comment on in the past two years."

Brett's eyes narrowed, but instead of warning Joe about insubordination the way he had every right to, he smiled. "Guess that would be a short list."

"Sorry," Joe said, as he dropped back into the chair. "I've just had some things on my mind."

Brett watched him too long not to be reading something into the conversation. The last thing Joe needed was to have the lieutenant realize he didn't have his head together on the job. Best friend or not, Brett would be duty-bound to speak up about it to the post commander, Kowalski, which would mean a psych consult that could waylay Joe's attempt to make sergeant.

"This wouldn't have anything to do with a certain redhead who was in here the other day, would it?" Brett asked finally.

"Why do we even have police radios or laptops or cell phones when we have Clara to keep communication flowing?" Blowing out a frustrated sigh, Joe looked over to Brett, who was grinning at him.

"What?"

"I happened to be in the office myself that day." Brett held his hands wide. "I do occasionally hang around this place. I have to put in a few hours if I'm going to get that the cushy state workers' pension."

"Oh. Right."

"So…Lindsay Collins. Age twenty-eight. Wixom."

The side of Joe's mouth lifted despite his best effort to keep his face blank. "Guess you haven't forgotten how to read a police report."

"Guess not." But then Brett's expression became serious. "It's always a tough case when there's a loss of life."

Joe could see the wheels turning inside Brett's head, the same wheels that served the lieutenant well on an investigation.

"Miss Collins came to you for…?"

"Answers," Joe said, completing his sentence. "She can't remember what happened in the accident that you read about, and she asked me to fill in some of the blanks."

"And were you able to…help?" Brett's serious expression broke into a grin as he said the last.

"That's what we're supposed to do," Joe grumbled, his jaw tight. "Help people."

"It had to be a hardship to come to the aid of a lovely woman like that, but somebody had to do it, right?"

"Knock it off, Lancaster. I mean…sir." Joe cleared his throat. "Look, Miss Collins is just a victim in a case I investigated. That's it. I told you I'm not even doing the dating thing right now. With anyone." *And certainly not with her,* he somehow managed not to add.

"Funny. I didn't mention dating."

Joe frowned. Brett didn't appear to be buying anything he said, but he couldn't blame him. Joe didn't have much credibility regarding women after so many years as a confirmed bachelor. He'd also always been able to take a joke before, so this new sensitivity was telling.

"Whatever." He rolled his eyes. "She just needed help with the accident details, and then she was named guardian of her late sister's child, and she needed some support—"

"The kids always get to guys like us, don't they?"

"What?" Joe was relieved for the interruption to his rambling that could only confirm that Lindsay Collins was part of his problem, but when the meaning of Brett's words dawned on him, he grimaced. "You mean like you and Tricia?"

"Clara said Miss Collins's niece is a cute kid. And a legal guardian is almost like a mom—"

Joe shook his head to interrupt him. "I hate to tell you this, buddy, but most single guys aren't on a hunt for widowed mothers of three."

"Well, that's good because the most amazing one is off the market," Brett said with a self-satisfied grin. "And now we're the proud parents of five."

Which was a whole other crazy matter in Joe's opinion, but because he was the best man from their wedding, and he wanted to preserve that friendship, Joe kept that opinion to himself.

"Remember when you told me you couldn't be dragged to the altar by anything less threatening than a howitzer?" Brett said with a chuckle.

"And don't you hate supposed friends who use your old comments against you?" He shook his head. "Look, I think you and Tricia are great, but I'm telling you that a woman is not *my* problem." At least not all of it.

Brett shook his index finger at him and squinted as if deep in thought, but then he opened his eyes as if he'd found his answer. "Then it has to be the sergeant test that's bugging you. Don't worry about it. You're ready. You've been ready for a long time. You should have taken this step years ago."

"You're right about that."

It didn't surprise him that the lieutenant had hit on a part of his problem. He was only relieved that Brett hadn't figured out the rest. He couldn't afford to let anyone know, especially not Brett, that he'd lost his confidence out on patrol. They couldn't know that he was a liability to the other men and women on the force.

Brett had already guessed that Lindsay was a part of his problem, too, and whether she was the problem or just a reminder of it, he should have been backing away from her instead of becoming friends. A rational man who wanted to keep his job and his family legacy would do what needed to be done, but when had he ever been rational? No matter what he should do, he knew what he *would* do, and that was to show up to meet her as planned.

That truth only frustrated him more. If he didn't figure this out, his superiors would figure *him* out, or worse, something unthinkable could happen while he was out on patrol. A feeling deep in his gut told him it was only a matter of time.

"Why isn't Trooper Joe here, Aunt Lindsay?"

Lindsay looked up to find Emma pouring another bucket of water into her castle's moat. The child, who laughed and played in her daisy-covered tankini, didn't appear to have any lasting effects from her nightmare the night before. She didn't even seem to mind that the water she poured into her moat was only absorbed into the sand.

"I don't know." Lindsay smeared on another layer of sunscreen as she sat on a blanket just beyond the reach of the tide's tiny ripples. "Maybe something came up."

At least, that was the only way Lindsay could explain it. Joe had definitely said he was planning to come and hadn't called to cancel, so she didn't know what to think. She pulled her cell phone from where she'd tucked it beneath a beach towel and shielded the screen with her hand. No missed call. No text message.

"But he promised." Emma's lips were pursed in a pout. "He always keeps his promises."

"I never said promise." Lindsay didn't know why she bothered trying to explain. If she'd learned anything in the past few weeks, it was that Emma took anything she said as a promise. If only she'd left Joe's plan to meet them as a surprise, then Emma wouldn't have to think that he'd stood her up. Just the way Lindsay felt.

"You could only be stood up if it was a real date," she said under her breath and then shook her head.

It had never been a date. Was that what she'd really been looking for when she'd invited him? Of course not. They were friends, new ones, and that was all. She could admit to being lonely and even to being nervous when she'd invited him, but she was still convinced that she'd asked him for a better reason than to improve her nonexistent social life. This was for Emma.

It was a practical decision. Rather than to continue rejecting his offers of help, she'd chosen to welcome them. Joe would be a good resource, and she'd planned to glean as much information as she could about caring for Emma during their day at the beach. Unfortunately, Joe had demonstrated instead how unreliable people could be. Maybe she deserved his no-show for choosing to rely on someone else instead of being independent the way she should have been.

"I want him to come," Emma whined.

"I know you do, sweetie."

"He can take me to the sprinklers park."

Lindsay looked over at the gated, mini water park, only about a thousand feet away from their spot on the beach. She shouldn't have mentioned they could possibly go there, either. Now whatever they did would be a disappointment instead of an adventure.

"Live and learn," she blew out on a frustrated sigh.

"Learn what?"

At the sound of Joe's voice, Lindsay felt a tingle creep up her spine. Shifting her arm behind her, she turned to see him crossing the sand, wearing a pair of long red-and-blue swimming trunks, topped by a white Northern Michigan University T-shirt. That her mouth went dry just watching his approach brought her whole "just friends" premise into question. Serious question.

Only, something wasn't right about the way he

crossed the grass area with that long stride and sharp whip of his arms. She couldn't help but notice the hard set of his jaw as he stopped at the edge of her blanket, but she didn't miss, either, the way his gaze paused on her and that he swallowed visibly as he looked away.

"You're here," she managed to choke out.

Joe cleared his throat. "I said I would come today, didn't I?"

"Yes, but—"

Lindsay wasn't sure what she would have said next, but she didn't have the chance as Emma looked up from her castle masterpiece, dropped her shovel and threw herself at a certain state trooper, sandy feet and all.

"Trooper Joe, ya came," Emma said with delight.

"Of course I did. I always keep my promises."

The child turned back to her aunt. "See, I told you."

That Joe didn't even look back at Lindsay as Emma dragged him over to the sand castle made her uncomfortable. What was up with him?

"Look at my castle," Emma said. "I built it myself."

"Hmm. I'd better get a good look at this." Joe crouched down and took his time examining the creation that bore more resemblance to a lopsided igloo on an iceberg than any palace with a drawbridge. "You did all of this stuff? It's amazing."

Emma nodded, beaming, and described her creation for him in great detail. Lindsay couldn't help smiling as Joe paid close attention to the child, pointing, mostly in error, to the parts she described. When Joe looked back to Lindsay, and his jaw tightened, she decided that despite his efforts to hide it, something wasn't right.

Finally, Joe stepped on the edge of the blanket to protect his feet from the hot sand.

She glanced up and caught him watching her again, his gaze narrowed.

"When are you going to tell me what's wrong?"

"Why would there be anything wrong?" But he didn't look at her as he said it.

"I expected you a little earlier. Did something happen at work, or did we get our signals crossed?"

He shook his head. "Paperwork. That's just part of police work. The boring part of the job."

"If you get this worked up over the boring part, then I'd hate to see you after you deal with something serious."

She'd just been joking to lighten his mood, but she regretted the words as soon as she'd spoken them. How could she have forgotten, even for a minute? She was one of the people he'd met during one of those serious moments, and whether she could recall the event or not, he'd *carried her* to safety. She swallowed.

Joe was watching her, as if he was waiting for her to make that connection. He nodded over her reaction.

"I always have to be ready for those times. Always have to be sharp. On my toes."

With each comment, his jaw flexed tighter, and his gaze seemed to bore further through her. It was obvious that he was frustrated, but she wasn't sure why. Could it involve whatever he wasn't telling her about the accident? She swallowed. What exactly had she done, and why wouldn't he tell her?

"Distractions are unacceptable," he continued. "They can't happen. My hesitating could get somebody killed."

His gaze met hers again, and they locked in a solemn connection. Neither mentioned that lives could be and had been lost in his work, even when he didn't hesitate. That truth was a like an elephant sitting right there on the beach with them—between them. But Lindsay couldn't let the silence stretch any further, crawling under her skin and disturbing the bits of peace and acceptance she'd fought so hard for in the past six months, so she asked one of the questions clamoring for answers.

"Did you feel distracted this morning at work after…last night?"

He opened his mouth to answer, but she rushed on, suddenly afraid of what he might say.

"Because I'm sorry. I shouldn't have called you. I should have either handled the situation myself or have bit the bullet and called my parents. My not wanting to lose face with them was no excuse for me to ask you for help."

But he was shaking his head as he lowered himself to sit on the edge of the blanket, so Lindsay stopped, giving him a chance to answer.

"You should never have to be afraid of reaching out to a friend when you need help."

"You said that's what we are, but are you sure you meant it?"

"Why wouldn't I have?" He shifted, and instead of meeting her gaze, he looked over to Emma, who was still hard at work on her castle.

"Then why did you suggest that Emma and I are distractions rather than friends?"

Squeezing his eyes shut, he shoved a hand through his short hair. "That's not what I meant. I just—" He stopped himself, shaking his head. "I don't know what I meant. I'm tired, I guess, and cranky."

"I wasn't going to mention that."

His expression softened as he looked back at her again. "Thanks. I would expect you to be surly today as well, but you're all sunshiny. And look at her." He indicated Emma with a tilt of his head. "She's no worse for the wear."

"Well, Emma and I had the chance to sleep while you were out fighting crime on Michigan highways. I don't know how you were able to pull it together at six a.m."

"Obviously, I didn't do such a good job of it." He smiled. "I was just so off today that I worried I would make a mistake. I couldn't afford—"

He broke off, but Lindsay couldn't stop herself from filling in for him. "To make another one?"

His eyes widened, but he didn't answer.

"You can't blame yourself for what happened the day of the accident."

"I don't," he said finally.

"Don't you?"

His only answer was a shrug.

"You did everything you could." Except to pull her sister from the car first, but she wouldn't say that to him now. It was her issue, not his.

"Sometimes it's just not enough."

"Are we back to that again?" She'd said almost the same thing last night when they'd been talking about her caring for Emma.

"I guess we are."

He was grinning when she met his gaze, and then, as if they'd planned it, they glanced at Emma at the same time.

"She's a great kid." Lindsay couldn't help smiling as she watched her niece. "I'm going to give her the best life I can, no matter what I have to do."

"Even if it means hanging out with a guy like me?"

"I keep saying that you offered."

"And I keep admitting that I did, but sometimes…" He let his words trail away as he grinned at her.

"You wish you didn't?" She put her hand to her mouth in mock horror. "And I was ready to admit that you just might be able to teach me a few things about kids."

"Well, don't go and admit something like that or I'll get all overconfident. You don't want to be responsible for that."

"Oh, no." She shook her head slowly. "I'll just keep that information to myself, then."

"As long as that's settled." He paused and then added, "You know, I don't really know that much about kids."

"More than I do, but that doesn't take much. Emma adores you, too, and it's not completely horrifying having you around, so…"

"That's good because I'm not horrified being here."

Staring at the ground, Lindsay became serious. "It's beyond the range of your duties to spend time with accident victims, so I'll understand if you want to go now, or if you don't want to accept any other invitations."

He cleared his throat, so Lindsay figured whatever he said next would be something she didn't want to hear. But then he grinned.

"You got me to come all the way here, and now you're uninviting me?"

She shook her head. "No, that's not what I—"

But his suddenly serious expression stopped her.

"We're new friends, so there are things you don't know about me. But I'm going to tell you one right now." He took a deep breath and continued. "I am never anywhere I don't want to be."

Chapter Seven

She shouldn't stare. Lindsay knew that. But she couldn't make herself look away from the man who'd just spoken the most significant words any man had ever said to her. She didn't even mind that he was only doing it for Emma. She was relieved that someone else cared for Emma's well-being as much as she did and was willing to invest time to ensure that her needs were met.

But then Joe looked back at her, and their gazes touched in a connection as warm as it was confusing. She felt as if she'd been sunburned from the inside out. His smile drew her in, helplessly yet willingly. Her breath caught, and she lost the ability to blink.

Okay, she didn't have a huge frame of reference, just a select group of male friends, but she'd been able to look away from all of them. With Joe, she didn't even want to, and since time seemed to have stopped, she didn't have to force herself.

"Look, Aunt Lindsay. Look, Trooper Joe. I buried my feet."

Lindsay blinked as a three-year-old interrupted that pause in space and time. Her castle forgotten, Emma sat just off the blanket, her feet covered under mounds of sand.

"Well..." Lindsay paused to clear her throat "...you sure did. I can't even tell where they are."

"They're right here, silly." She wiggled until ten little pink toes peeked up through the sand.

"Oh, I can see some feet now." Joe popped up and scrambled over so he could tickle Emma's feet.

Lindsay struggled to pull herself up from the blanket, her cane providing little leverage in the sand. Jumping up, Joe reached out to steady her, but she waved away his offer with a brush of her hand. The last thing she needed right now would be to feel his touch on her arm and be tempted to lean into the strength of it.

Taking a few steps closer to Emma, she settled between the castle and the child's self-burial project. Lindsay moved her feet, the sand feeling like clay between her toes. That dank fish-and-seaweed smell, distinct to lake water, rose in her nose. She might have been tempted to think that something—or someone—had awakened all of her senses, but she chose to believe instead that she hadn't been paying attention before.

"I think Emma could use some help, don't you?" Joe winked at Lindsay and then plopped down next to them and started clumping damp sand over those protruding toes.

"You're right. She needs a lot of help."

Soon a giggling Emma was buried in the sand until her nose, eyes and mouth were her only visible parts.

"Should we let her out now?" Joe asked.

"I don't know," Lindsay said with a laugh. "I like her this way."

But Emma made a monsterlike sound and sat up, with the drier sand falling away from her skin and the damper parts sticking like messy brown glue.

"Looks like somebody needs a rinse," Joe said.

"Not me."

But Joe scooped her up anyway and started out into the murky waters of Kent Lake. Little girl giggles and hearty male laughter followed, as they negotiated the rocky shoreline and rolled around in knee-deep water, replacing some of that sand with seaweed.

Moving back to her blanket, Lindsay leaned back on her elbows to watch them, occasionally brushing at the perspiration at her temples. There were other groups on the beach, as well—teenagers playing volleyball, young women in bikinis soaking up the rays and a couple with a baby who cried every time he got his feet wet.

Lindsay didn't know how long she'd sat there watching, but suddenly her mind had changed the story behind the people out in the water. It wasn't hard at all for her to picture Joe, Emma and herself as a warm and happy family of three. When Joe would come out of the water, Lindsay would hand him a fluffy towel so he could wrap Emma in it. Then he would shift the child to Lindsay and pull both woman and child into the safety and comfort of his arms.

Would he brush a kiss over Emma's head and then turn to touch his lips to Lindsay's? She swallowed, even as her lips tingled over the thought. What was she thinking? How had she allowed her thoughts to veer so far from reality? How had she gone from recognizing that Joe was a kind man, who was helping them because of guilt over the accident, or pity for her orphaned niece or some other reason she didn't understand, to imagining a romance between them?

Lindsay must have messed up more than her hip socket joint in the accident if she was allowing herself to become attracted to Joe Rossetti. He was motivated by guilt. She'd accepted his offer of help, partially because she wanted answers and partially because she wasn't in the position to turn down any offer, but she couldn't allow herself to read more into their new friendship.

She was talking about Joe Rossetti, anyway. No matter how gorgeous and kind he was, and no matter how justified his reasons for making a split-second decision at an accident scene, the truth remained that he'd chosen between Lindsay and Delia. What kind of sister would even consider becoming involved with a man who'd made a choice like that? How could she betray Delia's memory that way?

"Come in with us, Aunt Lindsay," Emma called out to her, drawing her back from the faraway place to which her thoughts had traveled.

"Yeah, sunbathing beauty, aren't you coming out to play? Afraid you'll mess up your hair?"

She understood that he was kidding. Yet a flush climbed up her neck over his compliment. Did he think she was pretty? She shook her head, knowing she shouldn't care. When was she going to stop reacting like a silly schoolgirl around Joe Rossetti?

"This hair?" She patted the mess of it piled on top of her head. "I don't think you could mess this up."

"Then come on in," he said.

"Please, Aunt Lindsay."

Glancing at her cane and then to the rocky edge of the water, Lindsay shook her head. "I don't know."

But she used the cane to struggle to her feet anyway. She decided to leave on her cover-up over her swimsuit. She wanted to do this for Emma, but she couldn't take the cane in with her, and she was flustered enough around Joe without having to fall on her face in the water.

"Do you think she needs some encouragement, Emma?"

"Yeah. Let's go get her."

She braced herself as Joe and Emma climbed out of the water and jogged over to her. Joe wrapped a wet hand around Lindsay's waist, leaving her with no choice but to put her arm around his shoulder. Emma clutched Lindsay's other hand and pulled her toward the water, missing that Joe was supporting most of her aunt's weight.

Joe leaned around and looked down at Emma, just as they reached the water's edge. "You see? We talked her into it."

With the combined scents of lake water and masculine male flooding her senses, Lindsay had to concentrate on the damp chill of the swimmers sandwiching her to stay focused on the ten steps into the green water. After a few precarious seconds, as they stepped over the sharp rocks at the water's edge, they reached a sandy bottom in a shallow spot and stopped to let the tide rush past their knees.

"Thanks," Lindsay said in a low voice. It was important to her that she be able to participate in physical activities with Emma, and Joe had seemed to understand that without her saying so.

"Anytime."

His gaze caught hers again and held, but this time she had to look away. The image was too much like her fantasy. It made her long for things she'd never realized she wanted, things she couldn't allow herself to think about, when her focus needed to be on her niece who had lost so much. Lindsay glanced down at the sweet little girl holding her hand, but Emma pulled away and started running circles around the two adults.

"You can't catch me," she sang.

Lindsay braced herself, preparing to find her balance when Joe released her to chase after the child in the shallow water, but he kept his arm on her waist, his touch a warm reassurance that he wouldn't let her fall. Again, Lindsay rejected the temptation to see more than was there. Emma continued to run around and around them until she became dizzy and fell back into the water laughing.

Lindsay could relate to that feeling of being off-balance. The rational part of her was onboard with the idea that she should avoid thinking of anything beyond friendship with Joe. But that irrational part, the one that wanted things it shouldn't, was going to be harder to convince. Right now that disobedient part didn't want Joe Rossetti to let her go.

"Let me see those prune piggy toes."

Joe sat up from the place on the blanket where he'd dropped to rest what had felt like only seconds ago. Minutes or hours might have passed, but he'd been too content to notice. He breathed in the smells of the water, the foliage and the peace that seemed to have its own scent and exhaled a calm that he hadn't felt in a long time.

From the other side of the blanket where they'd sandwiched Emma between them, Lindsay chuckled. "No way, buddy. You leave my prune toes alone."

Joe glanced over in time to see Lindsay sit up and tuck her feet beneath a layer of sand. He didn't have to see them to know that she had coral-colored polish on her pretty toes any more than he needed to see her face to know she would be blushing after what she'd said. Yes, he was supposed to notice details in his job, but it was over-the-top for him to note that her nail color matched the hue that she often wore on her lips.

"Trooper Joe was talking about *my* toes." Emma

kicked both legs up into the air and wiggled all ten of them.

"Was I?"

He certainly hoped he was because he wouldn't be able to explain anything else. He was still trying to process the rush of feelings he'd experienced when helping Lindsay in the water. It wasn't just the experience of touching her, which he'd already learned had its own electrical charge, but knowing she trusted him was exhilarating.

Joe nabbed one of Emma's feet and squeezed a plump little toe. He shook his head. "Oh, this is much worse than I thought. We have some serious pruning here."

The worried look on Emma's face as she pulled her foot away made him laugh. He ruffled her hair. "I think they'll be fine, that is, if you spend some time out of the water."

"But the sprinkler park..."

Joe shook his head. "Nope. That can't happen today. Those toes need a rest. And let me get a look at those fingers." He reached for her tiny hand and turned it palm up before lifting it to show Lindsay. "Did you see these? I think a break from swimming is called for here."

Lindsay shook her head sadly. "I have to agree."

"We'll have to do that another day," he said, as Emma's lips formed a pout.

"It's time for us to be getting home anyway," Lindsay said.

"I don't want to—"

Lindsay held her index finger to her lips until the child stopped. "Remember, I told you we could get ice cream on the way home, but only if you could leave without complaining."

"Chocolate-and-vanilla twist? And not a baby cone."

The side of Lindsay's mouth lifted. "A small."

"Small is big."

The idea of a frozen treat winning over the tantrum, Emma stood up from the towel and started gathering her sand toys. As the child moved over to her deserted castle to collect her shovel and pail, Joe leaned in toward Lindsay.

"What were you saying about bribes?" He couldn't help grinning as he said it.

"They work sometimes. Anyway, this is an incentive program."

He nodded, but he couldn't keep a straight face. "You see? I did teach you something about kids."

"Now you've created a monster," Lindsay said with a frown as she struggled to stand up and then started shaking out the beach towels. "Two, if you're including Emma in that. Before long, I'll be bribing her with a sports car just to keep a C average on her report card."

"If you're handing out sports cars, would you

mind adopting me? I'll just go back to college. I'm sure I can find something else to study."

"I'll get right on it."

Emma raced back to them, her toys already in the mesh bag with sand trailing out through the holes. "Can Trooper Joe come with us to get ice cream?"

Lindsay glanced sidelong at him, as if waiting for his nod. When he gave it, Lindsay turned back to Emma. "If he wants to come, fine."

"Want to get ice cream, Trooper Joe?" Emma asked.

"I like ice cream."

Why was it that he suddenly wished Lindsay had invited him herself? It was just ice cream. But what he needed to admit to himself, even if he wouldn't confess it to anyone else under direct questioning, was that he wasn't ready to leave Lindsay Collins and her young niece just yet.

He didn't know how he'd gotten to this place. He'd been a mess at work, even after Brett had spoken to him, and he'd come here wound so tightly that even Lindsay had pointed it out. Yet, after a few minutes here with the two of them, all of his stress had melted away. That truth alone should have set off more bells in his mind than a four-alarm fire, but he didn't even have the good sense to be on high alert.

Didn't he realize that at any time she might start

asking questions again? Spending time with them, it was easy for him to blank out the memory of the accident that had brought them together in the first place, but it was wrong to keep the truth from Lindsay.

She had every right to know the whole truth, but he still didn't know how to tell her that he'd not only played God by choosing which sister would live, but that he'd refused to listen when she'd begged him to save her sister instead. He had to tell her; that was all there was to it. He just had to find the right time.

As Lindsay finished with the towels, Joe grabbed the blanket, shook it out and folded it over his arm.

"Here, let me get those." He reached for the pile of towels stacked on the sand, and then he took the ones she was already carrying from her arms.

"I am perfectly capable of doing this stuff myself."

"I know you are."

She'd taken a few steps toward the parking lot, but she stopped and looked back at him with a guarded expression, as if she expected him to make a joke. "I might move at a snail's pace, but I eventually get there."

"You're doing just fine." He meant more than about navigating a day at the beach, and she must have guessed that because she nodded, her gaze off to the side rather than meeting his. "You were doing just fine without any tips from anyone. Even me."

"Thanks."

Something must have caught her attention because her head turned and she focused on a bank of trees. Within seconds, a pair of runners emerged from the wooded area on the bike path, matching each other's stride.

"They're moving at a fast clip," she said when she caught him watching her.

"You really miss it, don't you?"

"Running?" She shrugged. "There's nothing I can do about that, at least until I've healed more. What am I supposed to do, try to run using a cane? That sounds like a disaster waiting to happen."

"But would you start running again if you could? And you did say that you're relying on your cane less and less, right?" He glanced at the sandy beach and looked back to her. "Except at the beach."

"It just isn't a possibility right now. I'm not confident enough in my balance to even attempt to run. And if I were ready again, I would still have to find child care for Emma while I ran. I don't know my neighbors that well, and after last night, they're probably not going to volunteer to baby-sit."

"But you would if you could, right?"

She gave an exasperated sigh. "I would if I could."

Her face was so sad that he was sorry he'd mentioned it and even sorrier that he'd pushed the issue. He'd rubbed salt in one of her open wounds from the accident, this one on the inside where no one could see. She must have wanted to escape the sting of it because she suddenly took a few steps away from him, stopping where Emma had set her bags of toys and was playing again in the sand.

"Okay, sweetie. We're really going to go now." She looped the mesh bag over her shoulder and took Emma's hand, relying a little on the cane in her other hand.

Joe helped them load the car and followed them in his truck to the ice-cream stand just outside the park entrance. He hoped they would make their stop a quick one. It wasn't as if he suddenly wanted to put some space between them, but the idea he'd just come up with was going to require him to be away from them for a while.

No, he couldn't take back the accident or restore Lindsay's family, but there was one thing he could return to Lindsay that she'd lost that day. He would help her to run again…with him. And maybe somewhere along the way he would find the courage to tell her the whole truth.

Chapter Eight

Lindsay closed her eyes as she sat on the front steps of her condo and tilted her head to feel the sun's warmth on her face. She relished a brief moment of peace. Today had been a series of rushes added to the serial scrambles of the past few weeks, from home to the day-care center to work, and the same list of stops in reverse.

So this was what parenting was really like. Not those tissue-inspiring moments, like on TV commercials. Day after day, doing the right thing. The responsible thing. It was tough, sometimes draining. She'd been told it was rewarding, too, but she hadn't experienced that part yet.

Opening her eyes, she twisted her body to look over her shoulder to the closed door behind her. Usually, by this time in the afternoon she would be hurrying to prepare dinner, but her effort would have been wasted today, since Emma had dozed off on the couch a half hour before. They were only having hot dogs and macaroni and cheese, anyway.

Lindsay dropped her head into the cradle her hands had formed as she rested her elbows on her knees. She was a failure as a guardian on so many levels. Emma had only been living with her for a few weeks, and already Lindsay had resorted to feeding her junk just to keep the peace at dinner. And letting Emma nap this late in the afternoon would make it nearly impossible to enforce her 8:30 bedtime.

As she stared out into the street, she could almost see the approval disappearing from her parents' eyes. At church the day before, her mother had told her it was a "good idea" when she'd described her plan for creating a regular schedule for Emma. A schedule she was already blowing.

You should give yourself a break. Lindsay bristled as Joe's words slipped into her thoughts uninvited. She didn't need him as her cheerleader here, but worse than that, she didn't need to be thinking about him one more time today. She shoved her hands back through her hair.

Wasn't she having a tough enough time balancing work and parenting roles without wasting time wondering why Joe hadn't called in two days? She shouldn't have been thinking about anyone at work, where her concentration needed to be on measuring gestational age and development on the ultrasound screen. She definitely shouldn't have been thinking about Joe.

He'd certainly managed to remove her from his thoughts, if the past few days were any indication. She hadn't seen or heard from him since Saturday. She shook her head. That couldn't matter to her… even if it did.

Straightening, Lindsay glanced out into the street again, looking for some entertainment. In this unique area of town, where modest older homes with established trees shared space with her newer condo complex, there was always someone out on the street, staying active. She used to be one of them.

As if to prove her point, a pair of in-line skaters raced on the asphalt, their arms pumping furiously with the effort to get the edge. A helmeted cyclist in racing gear passed them on the left. She followed the biker's path with her gaze, appreciating his joy for speed, his commitment to the sport.

When he was finally out of sight, she turned her head the opposite way, catching sight of a runner approaching in the distance and pushing a jogging stroller. Runners were always the hardest to watch, their freedom and fluid movements making her wish for things she couldn't have right now, so she turned away.

But curiosity drew her gaze back to the runner, who wore a baseball cap low over his eyes. Because he was closer now, just beyond the first condominium building, she got a better look at him. And his empty stroller. Lindsay rubbed her eyes and looked again, just to make sure her vision wasn't playing tricks on her.

She was still wondering why a tall, broad-shouldered man who didn't have the lean build of a runner, would be running up her street pushing an empty stroller, when he came into view. Her breath caught. A chill she couldn't explain scaled her arms, though it was probably seventy-five degrees outside.

Joe? Maybe red-faced, but that could be him, right? She gritted her teeth, shaking her head. It had been bad enough that she'd been thinking about him at work, but was she going to start seeing him everywhere now? Then the man she'd almost convinced herself was only a mirage grinned and waved. After he stopped the stroller on her driveway behind her car, he gripped its padded handle and bent at the waist, gasping for breath.

Grabbing her cane from beside the step, she made her way over to him. "Are you okay?"

Joe took a few more deep breaths, still bent over and holding up his index finger in an unspoken request for her to give him a minute.

She couldn't wait that long. "What are you doing here?"

"Isn't it obvious?" he said as he straightened. "I'm out for a run. It's a great day for one, isn't it?"

"Nope. It is definitely not obvious what you're doing here ready to pass out on my driveway. The only thing that *is* obvious is you really aren't a runner." She paused, studying him. "Just look at you. I'm tempted to call an ambulance."

"Thanks. Way to beat a guy down while he's hyperventilating. Maybe I need more cardio."

But he was grinning as he said it, and his face was losing its sunburned look with each breath.

"So…?" Stepping back, she leaned against the bumper of her car and propped her cane next to her leg.

He set the parking brake on the jogger and slipped the safety strap from around his wrist before waving his hand over the stroller. "Surprise."

Lindsay looked from Joe to the stroller and then back to Joe. "That's for me?"

"Well, I don't have that much use for it, other than to have it drag me down the hill after I pass out, so if you could use it…" He let his words trail away, his face becoming serious. "You miss running. It's important to you. This is a way you could do it again. I just thought—"

Lindsay shook her head until he stopped, but

there was nothing she could do to halt the feelings that bombarded her thoughts. Frustration and gratitude and another feeling she couldn't define shot at her from different directions until she wasn't sure how to respond. No one had ever done something so kind for her before. Certainly not any man.

She'd never expected anyone to understand how much she missed running, how she craved that burn in her muscles and that brush of the wind on her face, but it seemed to register with Joe. Even if she couldn't accept his gift, she would never forget how special it made her feel.

"I'm sorry. I just can't accept a gift like that." She could hear the sadness in her voice, so she didn't try to convince herself that he would miss it.

"That?" He pointed to the jogger. "That's not a gift. I don't count anything I could pick up off an internet classified ad as a gift. This was more like a need fulfillment. I saw a need, and I figured out a way to fulfill it."

His explanation had her lips lifting. "I *needed* a running stroller?"

"Well, not needed exactly, but it could kill two birds with one exceptionally large, three-wheeled stone."

"Which two birds?"

"The get-you-running one and gotta-have-child-care one."

"Are those rare breeds?"

"Not quite extinct, but definitely endangered."

"Can't argue with that."

Even as she continued their silly banter, she reasoned through his logic and a bit of her own, already tasting the salty sweat of a good run on her lips.

"Gift or *need fulfillment* or whatever you call it, I still wouldn't be able to just accept it from you. I would have to repay you for it. Every penny."

"That's not necessary—"

"It is to me."

"Fine." His frown quickly turned into a grin. "But remember, my loans come with interest. One point above Prime Rate. And I don't tolerate late payments."

Lindsay shook her head, still smiling. Joe Rossetti was impossible and exasperating and frustrating and wonderful. He owed her and Emma nothing, and yet he was always doing nice things for them. She was trying to tell herself that this was just another one of those nice things, something really intended for Emma's sake, but the case was harder to make this time.

Could he really have done this just for her? Could he have feelings for her that went beyond friendship? No. She pushed the errant thought away. She shouldn't ruin a perfect moment with her friend by reading too much into what he'd done.

"I'm not even sure how it would work," she said finally.

"The doctor said you didn't really need your cane anymore, didn't she? It's just there for extra support."

Lindsay tapped the cane next to her. "My wooden security blanket."

"This would be like that, too. Just like having a shoulder to lean on."

Lindsay glanced sidelong at him, only to find him watching her. He didn't have to say it, but in these past few days, he'd become a strong shoulder for her and for Emma. That was the type of man Trooper Joe Rossetti was—someone who put his life on the line every day to benefit others. But he was also the man who'd chosen between her and Delia. She couldn't forget that. Otherwise, it would be just too easy for her to fall for him.

"Go faster, Aunt Lindsay."

Emma kicked her heels inside the jogger and threw her head back in delight as they rounded yet another corner.

"This is the fastest I can go, sweetie," Lindsay explained as she had several times before during their walk that had lasted closer to an hour than the thirty minutes they'd originally planned.

Still, as they began the return trip to Lindsay's condo, Joe felt tightness in his chest that had nothing to do with physical exertion this time. He didn't want the walk to end, but what was he supposed to do? He couldn't turn Lindsay into a marathon walker just because he wanted to spend more time with her. Them. He meant *them*.

"Remember, Emma, that Aunt Lindsay wanted to practice walking with the jogger first before she tried running." He reached over the side of the stroller and ruffled the preschooler's hair.

"But she practiced already," Emma insisted.

"That's true, but she'll need more practice. Like when you practice writing your name. She wants to get really good at it, like you are with your writing."

Joe glanced sidelong at Lindsay, who'd been even steadier than he'd hoped while walking behind the stroller, gripping the padded handlebar with both hands.

"Who knew that Emma had such a need for speed?" he said.

Lindsay grinned as she came to a stop next to him and pushed the parking brake. "And I thought she'd be worried about being H-U-N-G-R-Y."

Both shot glances at the child in the stroller, just making sure she hadn't mastered the skill of deciphering oral spelling yet. But the girl only rocked forward and backward in her seat, as if to get her chariot going again.

"You see?" He gestured toward the child. "Nothing to worry about."

They would have had a difficult time convincing Emma that she needed to wait until after dinner for their walk, anyway. When she'd awakened from her nap and discovered the new toy, she immediately wanted to try it out.

Lindsay glanced at the child and then at him again. "Guess not."

With her face flushed from the exertion of the brisk walk and escaped tresses from her ponytail curling around her face, Lindsay had never looked prettier to him. He wondered if she'd always been this happy when training before the accident, her shoes tapping out a rhythm, her breathing slow and steady.

He realized with a shock that he would do almost anything to keep her smiling like that.

"Well, you look about the same as I did when I ran up to your house earlier."

Her gaze narrowed, but then her expression softened. "Whew. I thought you were serious. My doctor wouldn't be happy with me if I started doing too much too fast."

"No. You look great. Really." Joe swallowed. It wasn't supposed to have come out like that. He sounded as if he was looking at more than how she was handling this new activity, and it would be hard for him to deny it.

Lindsay glanced at him, licking her lips nervously. An awkward silence lingered, and Joe searched for something to say to defuse the electricity sparking between them. It wasn't dark enough for the stroller to require more than its reflectors, but the current between them could have powered headlights without batteries.

"Go, dog, go." Emma pointed in the direction she wanted the jogger to move.

The adults chuckled, but Lindsay's was a nervous laugh.

Because Joe hated making her so uncomfortable, he changed the subject. "Didn't I see a book that said something like that in Emma's room?"

"It's called, strangely enough, *Go, Dog. Go!* It's her new favorite at bedtime."

"Go, dog, go," Emma repeated, louder this time.

"Oh, I think she meant it." Lindsay released the parking brake and started forward again.

"You're doing a good job with her, you know. She's adapting well."

"Thanks." She didn't look at him, but her eyes were suspiciously shiny.

"I'm glad this running thing is going to work out for you guys." He paused long enough to watch her movements, so much more fluid than they'd been with the cane. "You look happy when you're moving. Complete."

"Is it so obvious?" Instead of waiting for an answer, she continued, "You must really think I'm shallow. My sister dies, my niece loses her mother, and all I can think about is that I can't run anymore."

Joe reached out for the jogger's handle and pulled her to a stop.

"That isn't all you've been thinking about. You've been mourning the loss of your sister, and you've stepped up in every way possible to care for Emma. You've put yourself last in this situation. You probably always do that. But in this one thing, don't."

Lindsay's wide eyes and the strange look on Emma's face as she twisted in her harness to look up at them made it clear he'd said too much. He might as well have announced how amazing he thought she was. He released his grip on the handle, and Lindsay started forward again without looking over at him.

Finally, she chuckled. "You make me sound like Florence Nightingale or Mother Teresa or something. Like in Matthew 16:24, 'If any man would come after me, let him deny himself and take up his cross and follow me.'" She shook her head. "I can assure you I'm not as selfless as you think I am."

"There you go quoting scripture again."

"I have to do something with all those memory verses I learned in Sunday School. My quoting ability always makes me the life of the party."

The words of a few verses he'd memorized himself long ago filtered through his thoughts, but he tucked them away. He had a point to make. "All I'm saying is it's okay to miss something that was more than a *hobby* to you."

"You didn't buy that, huh?"

"All those ribbons gave you away. It took a lot of dedication and pain to earn those."

"Okay, you got me."

Lindsay started forward again, and the condo complex came into view in the distance. Joe searched for a way to stall her longer, but he'd already been doing that. If he kept at it, he would have to explain why. Even he didn't know the answer to that.

"Running was the one thing I did for myself," she said after a long time. "I always felt close to God as I ran, testing my body and listening for His guidance. I've felt guilty about missing running, especially with everything my family has lost, but not being able to get out there has left another void in my life."

"I know what you mean."

Joe could sense Lindsay's gaze on him as she

weighed his words, but her next comment surprised him.

"You do know, don't you? Earlier, you said something about running making me feel complete. How did you know?"

"I'm not suggesting that there weren't days when you had to force yourself to put on your running shoes. But once you were out on the road, didn't you know without a doubt that was where you were supposed to be?"

For a few seconds, Lindsay didn't answer, and when she finally did, her voice was thick with emotion. "It was exactly like that, but I still don't understand how you know that. Is there something you feel that way about?"

He didn't know whether it was her question or that he'd been waiting for her to ask it, but Joe found the words pouring out of him like volcanic ash during an eruption. "A void for me would be never to strap on a weapon again, never to pin on a badge and not to have the chance to serve the public again."

His chest squeezed. Was now the right time to tell her the rest of the story that still weighed on his heart? Should he tell her how the events from the night of the accident related to his own loss of confidence and his fear that he would lose the job that meant so much to him?

She swallowed visibly, as if she recognized that

he'd said something significant, even though she couldn't know what else he'd been tempted to tell. But then she smiled.

"And do you often 'feel the burn' in your work?"

"It was an analogy."

"If you say so," she said with a chuckle.

Part of him was relieved for the break she always gave him, and part was frustrated that she hadn't demanded to know more. It was long past time for him to tell her the rest of the story he'd kept from her, for his benefit as much as hers.

But it was so easy to walk along with Lindsay in companionable silence. This felt so right. And after he told her, things between them would never be right again.

Lindsay saved him from having to acknowledge he was a coward by stopping and staring up into the trees that formed an arch over the running trail.

"See what I mean?" she said. "You have to feel close to God out here, surrounded by His creations."

"I'm glad you have that if it helps you."

"Was it your mother's death that caused you to lose your faith?"

Joe blinked, surprised by the question. It wasn't a subject he enjoyed talking about, but even it was easier than the one he'd been considering. "I guess her death had something to do with it. She was definitely the strongest example of faith in our family. She was the one who corralled us together for church on Sunday mornings."

It had been years since he'd thought about his mother kneeling with him in prayer next to his bed, but now he could see it as clearly as if it were yesterday.

"She'd be disappointed to think that her death caused me to give up on God," he admitted.

"But you didn't."

"What do you mean?"

"If you didn't believe, you wouldn't have given me that poem."

"The poem? Are we back to that again?" He shook his head, rolling his eyes. "I told you it was an impulse to give it to you."

"Was it an impulse that made you carry a poem around in your trooper's hat? A poem that says, 'Don't be afraid. You are a child of God. You are precious in his eyes.'"

"No, it wasn't like that." Even as he said it, he wasn't sure. Had he on some level wanted to reclaim his faith, even if he wasn't ready to commit to it?

"I don't know why I kept the poem. My friend Cindy gave it to me and told me that a police officer gave it to her during the lowest point in her life. Her husband had left her. She'd lost her job, and then the officer stopped her for speeding. When she burst into tears and the whole story spilled out, he reached into his hat and pulled out the poem to give to her."

"Oh, that must have been an awful time for her," she said.

"It was. I still don't know why Cindy passed the poem to me."

Lindsay stared at him, a knowing look in her eyes.

"It probably just impressed me that the guy carried it in his hat, so I started doing the same."

"You think that was all it was?"

He frowned because even he was beginning to wonder. "I never intended to pass it along to anyone."

"But you did, and I'm glad you did. It reminded me that, like in Luke 1:37, 'For with God nothing will be impossible.'"

She smiled at him, and like he always did, he felt that smile all the way to his toes. But then, as she turned to look ahead again, something must have caught her attention because she jerked the jogger to a stop.

Parked behind Lindsay's car was a sedan he didn't recognize, with a driver still behind the wheel. He stiffened, but instead of feeling the instinct to touch his weapon that was still locked in its case back in his truck, he felt a territorial reaction.

Jealousy? That was ridiculous. He was never jealous. He had no business feeling that way over Lindsay, anyway. So why was he watching that car and hoping the driver didn't turn out to be younger or taller or better looking?

"Were you expecting someone?"

She shook her head.

"What is it?" He strained his eyes to get a better look. "A guy?"

"A man and a woman. They're my parents."

Chapter Nine

Lindsay straightened her shoulders and then pushed the stroller forward. She hadn't done anything wrong, and yet she felt guilty as she watched her father and mother open the doors and climb out of the car.

"They didn't say they were coming by," she told Joe, though he hadn't asked.

"It's Nannie and Papa," Emma called out with glee.

By the time they reached her driveway, Lindsay's parents were standing together, leaning against the driver's side of the car. Her mother had her arms crossed over her chest, and her father was twirling his keys.

"Well, there she is," her father said, as he bent down to get on Emma's level. He reached down and unbuckled the child from her harness and lifted her onto his hip.

"Hi, Mom and Dad," Lindsay said.

"Where have you been?" her mother asked her, while eyeing Joe suspiciously.

Her father was the first to step forward. "I don't think we've met."

"But…you have," Lindsay said, falling over her words as she locked the jogger's brake. She released the handle and stepped carefully toward the group of adults.

"Joe, these are my parents, Brian and Donna Collins."

"Mom and Dad, this is Trooper Joe Rossetti. You met…at the hospital."

Lindsay braced herself as her father stepped back from shaking hands with Joe. Usually, her mother was easiest to read, her anger or frustration obvious in her tight jaw or a flash in her eyes. But this time her father's annoyance was more obvious in the way he kept jangling his keys.

"Trooper Joe and Aunt Lindsay went running with me," Emma announced. "It wasn't very fast."

"I guess you ran for a long time because Nannie and Papa have been waiting here a whole hour," Donna said.

Her mother might have been talking to Emma as she let her gaze pass over the jogging stroller, but the message appeared to be for Lindsay alone.

"I'm sorry we made you wait."

Lindsay was sorry about a lot of things right

now, and that she'd been out running around, almost literally, when her parents had arrived at her home was just one of them. The annoyance she felt that her parents hadn't called first was another. This wasn't the first time since Emma had started spending the majority of her time at Lindsay's condo that her parents had shown up unannounced, and it probably wouldn't be the last.

Brian touched his forehead to his granddaughter's. "We tried to come just after dinner, so—"

"I'm hungry," Emma said, as though she'd just now realized it. "I want dinner."

"Dinner?" Donna lifted a shocked brow. "That poor child hasn't had dinner yet? It's nearly seven-thirty."

Lindsay shot a glance at Joe, who looked as uncomfortable as she felt, and then turned back to her mother. "I know it's a little late, but she fell asleep on the way home from day care. Then Joe came by with a jogging stroller, and—"

"Were you napping at almost dinner time, dear heart?" Donna stepped over to where Brian was holding Emma and brushed the child's hair back from her face. "Now you won't get any sleep tonight at all. You tell Aunt Lindsay not to let you nap so late anymore."

"Okay, Nannie."

Joe took a step forward. "I messed up the schedule tonight. Sorry about that, Lindsay." After he sent an apologetic look her way, he turned back to her parents.

"I was just so excited about the new toy I found that I had to bring it to Lindsay immediately," he continued. "Emma wanted to try it out right away. Did you see? Lindsay can already walk steadily with it. She'll be running with it in no time."

"Lindsay has more important responsibilities than running now," Brian told him. "She might not have as much free time for her hobbies anymore."

Joe opened his mouth, looking as if he was about to come to Lindsay's defense, when Emma made a tortured sound.

"I'm hungry," she moaned.

Donna reached up to touch her granddaughter's arm. "Here, Emma, you and I can run into the kitchen and see what we can make for a late dinner."

"Oh, don't worry about it, Mom," Lindsay said quickly. "We were planning to have something easy tonight. It will only take a few minutes."

"We're having hot dogs and macaroni and cheese," Emma announced, as if it was some great accomplishment.

"Oh" was all Lindsay's mother had to say about that. It was enough.

Lindsay pretended not to notice the odd exchange between her parents. Her father was the first to look back to her.

"Maybe Emma should spend tonight at our house. Wouldn't that be fun, Emma?"

"Can I, Aunt Lindsay?"

"Don't you remember?" Lindsay said, trying to force down the anxiety that gripped like a fist inside her chest. "You're going to Nannie and Papa's tomorrow and staying for two whole nights, so it would be best for you to wait until then."

The child appeared to think it through before she asked, "Can I bring Monkey Man and my pink suitcase?"

"Sure you can."

Lindsay let out the breath she was holding slowly, but she couldn't slow her racing pulse. It was to her benefit that Emma didn't yet have the reasoning skills to realize that her stay at her grandparents' house could have been extended from two days to three and then from one more to forever. Lindsay knew it only too well. If she'd learned nothing else from her accident, she knew that nothing was forever.

"I had better get inside and get started." She sent Joe an apologetic look and started backing away. "So, I guess I'll see you later."

Joe cleared his throat. "Oh. Right." He opened his mouth again, but he must have thought better of whatever he'd intended to say because he closed it again.

Relief flooded through Lindsay's veins. Had he been about to offer to stick around and face her parents with her? As much as she was grateful for the thought, it was about the last thing she needed. Her parents were already upset enough with her without adding that to the mix.

"Uh. Lindsay," he called after her when she was almost to the front door. "Do you want me to put the jogger on your deck until you plan for a place to store it?"

"Oh. Sure." She hadn't thought about storing it yet. Just as she hadn't thought about whether it was wise to delay dinner or let Emma nap too late or spend over an hour on a walk with a man she found too appealing for her own good. "Yes, the deck will be fine."

"I'll just drop it off and head out. See you later."

"Thanks so much." She wanted to say more, but how could she, when her parents were right there, listening to every word? She hated that after everything Joe had done for her, she would have to leave him to walk back to the library to pick up his truck. But what could she do?

With a wave, she started into the house, her mother following closely behind and her father taking up the rear and carrying Emma. Brian stopped by Emma's toy box in the living room and stayed there to watch the child play, while Donna followed Lindsay into the kitchen.

"What was that all about?" her mother said.

Lindsay cleared her throat as she turned back to her, switching the oven on to Broil for the hot dogs. "I don't know what you mean."

"You know perfectly well what I mean. You were on a *date* tonight when Emma hadn't even had dinner, and you were pushing her around in an expensive gift that you never should have accepted. And now that you're finally feeding her, you're giving her…that." She pointed to the boxed macaroni that Lindsay had set next to the stove.

"It wasn't a date," Lindsay answered in a low voice.

Her mother made a sharp sound in her throat, causing Lindsay to look up from the pot of water she was watching too closely for it ever to boil.

"Of all the things I just said, that's the one you chose to comment on?"

Lindsay stiffened, feeling transparent. How could she explain it to her mother when she couldn't even make sense of it herself? She'd made so many excuses lately about why she was spending so much time with Joe, and they all sounded empty now.

"I just wanted to clear that up." Lindsay wanted to stop there, knew it was enough. Yet the words kept bubbling like the water on the stove should have been but wasn't. "Joe—I mean Trooper Rossetti—found the jogging stroller online and thought it might help me out, so he bought it. I insisted on paying him back for it."

"Well, at least you did that."

"And the jogger really is great," Lindsay continued, unable to stop. "Emma loves it, too. It will be good for the two of us—Emma and me—to get some fresh air together."

Her mother only shook her head until Lindsay stopped talking.

"You've always been sensible about men before. Why would you pick now, of all times, to change that?"

Lindsay turned to put foil on the broiling pan to cover her surprise. "Mom, you're getting the wrong idea about us," she finally managed to say.

She wanted to believe it, too, but the fact that she was fighting back resentment over her mother's words gave no support to her argument. It hurt that what her mother called *sensibility* probably had been awkwardness around men, and it hurt even more to realize that Lindsay wished she could have been different this time. With Joe.

"Are you sure it's the wrong idea?"

"I'm sure. Really. It's not like that."

"How did you even come across Trooper Rossetti in the first place? We haven't seen him since—" Her mother's breath caught, and her eyes shone with another round of the many tears she'd cried over the past six months. "Since that night."

"His name was on the original police report, so I went to the state police post to ask him some questions. I thought he could fill in some of those blanks about the night that D...the night of the accident."

Would it ever get easier to talk with her mother about Delia's death? Would she ever get over feeling responsible for separating *two* mothers from their daughters?

"I told you that some stones are better left—"

"Unturned? That's what you've said, Mom, but these questions were making me crazy. I had to know."

"Fine. But how did you get from asking questions to gallivanting around the neighborhood with him, pushing Emma in a stroller?"

"We weren't gallivanting. It was just a walk."

But semantics aside, she couldn't blame her mom for asking because she wasn't entirely sure herself how she and Joe had reached that point. Maybe in the beginning, she'd been looking for answers and he'd been searching for absolution, but somehow they'd gone from there to laughing together and pushing a jogging stroller. She'd enjoyed the whole ride more than she wanted to admit.

"If you think you're keeping some big secret, that grin gives you away."

Lindsay hadn't even realized she was smiling, hadn't felt the expression slipping onto her face, but she removed it. What did it mean when she couldn't stop smiling when she thought of him?

"Mom, he's just a friend," she said, as much for her own benefit as her mother's. "He felt badly for us and was trying to do something nice. You always taught us to do things for other people. Why is it not okay for me to accept kindness from someone else?"

"Don't turn this around on me. We also taught you not to go accepting gifts from men."

"I said I was paying him back for it."

"Don't you get it?"

Lindsay jerked at the sharp tone of her mother's voice, and she swallowed as she turned to look at her.

"Have you thought for one minute about who this man is that you've invited to spend time with you and Emma?"

"Of course I've thought about it." In the beginning, she'd thought of little else, so it surprised her now to realize how long it had been since she'd let Joe's role in the accident matter to her.

"Then you have to remember how he came into your life? Into *our lives?*"

"No, Mom, I *don't* remember."

"Well, I do. I remember that young man in the soaked uniform walking up to us in the hospital hallway and telling us how sorry he was—" Her voice caught then, and she took a few steps away to the window so she could stare out at the darkening sky.

"Was Joe—I mean Trooper Rossetti—the first one to tell you...what happened?"

Her mother shook her head. "No, the officers who came to the house did that, but he met us at the hospital. Outside your room."

"Is that why it bothered you so much that he was here? Because he reminds you of that night?"

"That has nothing to do with it. *We* have nothing to do with it."

Lindsay doubted both of those claims, and her skepticism must have shown because her mother folded her arms over her chest. "This is about you. Delia put a lot of trust in you when she named you as Emma's guardian."

"I know that, Mom." Trembling inside, Lindsay poured the pasta into the finally boiling water and put the broiler pan in the oven, leaving the door partly open. "You know I'm honored that she thought of me."

"If you're as *honored* as you say, then I'm surprised that you're thinking about your social life—friends or whatever it is—when you should be focused on Emma."

Lindsay opened her mouth to argue the point, but then she closed it. Could she really say she'd been making Emma her top priority when she'd been spending so much time thinking about a certain state police trooper?

"But, Mom, I'm doing everything I know how to become the best caregiver I can be for Emma." At least she'd thought so, but now she wondered if it was true.

"Do you think Delia would agree?"

The words struck Lindsay with more force than a blow ever could have. Eyes burning, Lindsay turned away to pull the broiler pan from the oven. What would Delia think about the time Lindsay had been spending with a man instead of focusing on Emma? What would she think about *which* man?

As if she realized her comment had hit its mark, Donna reached for the pan on the stove and poured the cooked pasta into the colander in the sink. "Let's get this…dinner on the table before the child starves."

"Did someone say dinner?" Brian said as he came into the room with Emma on his back.

"Dinner!" Emma lifted a fist into the air as her grandfather lowered her to the ground.

Lindsay's thoughts flashed back to another recent dinner, one with just as much tension, but ultimately a lot more laughter. But the fact that she remembered that dinner *now* only frustrated her more. Even after her mother had pointed out that she needed to get her focus in the right place, she still couldn't get Joe out of her mind.

"Would anyone else like to eat?" She quartered the hot dogs to avoid a choking hazard and waited for her parents' polite refusals. "Okay then. Dinner for one coming up."

"She really was hungry," Brian said as they watched the child eating with gusto.

"I love hot dogs," Emma announced, waving her little fork in the air. "Mommy liked hot dogs."

For the span of a few seconds, Lindsay and her parents exchanged looks that mirrored the pain and loss they all shared, but then the child started talking again.

"With ketchup. Yuck."

Emma made a face to match her sentiment. Lindsay's chest squeezed, and she blinked back tears.

"You know, I didn't remember that about your mommy, but you're right." Lindsay paused to clear her throat and forced a smile. "She did like hot dogs and ketchup. You'll have to tell me more things about her, and I'll tell you more stories about when she was a little girl."

"Can you tell me some stories at bedtime?"

"Absolutely. So get your pajamas, and I'll be right up to give you your bath."

Lindsay waited, expecting Emma to argue or to ask again to spend the night at her grandparents' house, but she popped out of the chair and rushed out of the room.

"She was in such a hurry, she forgot to kiss us good-bye." Brian smiled. "Maybe someone has her priorities in order after all."

"I do, Dad."

Well, if she hadn't had them in order before, this was the wake-up call she needed. Emma had to come first. And if putting her niece first meant creating distance between herself and the friend who'd come to mean so much to her in a short time, then she would do it.

Sure, she'd thought she might be able to help Joe reclaim his faith, but she was probably as unqualified to help with that as her parents worried she was to be Emma's guardian. And her plan to convince him to tell her what he was keeping from her about the accident...well, maybe her mother was right about leaving some stones where they were.

Lindsay glanced outside to the last place she'd seen Joe, and her breath hitched. If keeping her distance from Joe Rossetti was the right thing to do for Emma and for herself, then why did just the thought of it hurt so much?

Chapter Ten

Joe pressed his ear to his phone as Lindsay's cell rang once and then a second time. She hadn't automatically sent his call to voice mail this time, but he didn't hold out much hope that she would answer, or even if she did, that she wouldn't immediately shut him down. He knew what was happening, and he had a pretty good idea why.

The phone clicked after the fourth ring, so he waited for the call to go to voice mail. What did it say about a guy that he was tempted to listen to a voice-mail greeting just to hear a woman's voice, and when had he become *that guy?*

"Hello?"

His pulse leaped at the sound of her live voice. He cleared his throat. "Lindsay?"

"Oh, Joe. I didn't realize it was you."

"Forgot to check your caller ID this time."

"No, that's not—I mean I didn't—oh, whatever," she said with a nervous laugh.

"Now that we have *that* settled…" He chuckled. "So how has your week been going?" He wouldn't tell her his had been the loneliest since…well… ever.

"It hasn't been a week. I talked to you two days ago."

"Oh, you mean the time that you turned down my offer to take you and Emma out for ice cream?"

The sound she made was some combination of a cough and a laugh. "And we talked two days before that."

"You mean the time I asked you if you wanted to go running—I mean walking—again, and you said Emma was tired and you needed to make sure she got to bed on time?"

"That's not…"

It didn't surprise him that she didn't finish her thought. Both of them knew she was kicking him to the curb, which would be a difficult job since they weren't even dating, but she was doing it anyway. What was far less clear to him was why it bothered him so much.

"You probably think I'm dense by now," he said. "I was supposed to get the hint, especially after all of those 'missed' calls."

Something had changed from the moment Lindsay had come home to find her parents waiting for her with disappointment in their daughter and distrust of her friend painted on their faces.

"Come on. It isn't like that."

He wanted to know what it *was* like, wished she would tell him what her parents had said the other night to make her avoid him, but asking her would be like begging her to hang up on him. Then he wouldn't be able to even try out his new plan. The one that just might work.

"Don't worry," he said. "I know rejection when I hear it." He also knew what a challenge was like. That had to be what kept him asking when he could have simply slunk away, discarded.

"It's just that, well, I really have been busy."

"Washing your hair?"

She cleared her throat. "No, Joe. I'm been busy being Emma's guardian."

"I know. How's she doing?" He felt as if he was speaking in code, asking about the child, when his real questions were about her aunt.

"She's fine. Really."

"I miss her."

"She misses you, too," she answered, in a quiet voice.

Something tightened in his throat, but then it struck him that he was the only one talking in code about the two of them, and she was probably *really* referring to Emma. Silence stretched between them so long that he wondered whether the call had been dropped, but then she sighed loudly into the receiver.

"Look. Thanks for calling, but it's getting late and I'd better—"

"It's only eight forty-five on a Saturday night, and you probably already have Emma in bed." He paused long enough for her to tell him he was wrong, but when she didn't, he started again. "I have a question to ask you anyway."

"Joe, are we going to keep doing this?"

"I don't know what you're talking about," he said lightly. "Here I was, just trying to invite you and Emma to church, and you seem to think I have some ulterior motive."

"Church?" Her voice dripped with skepticism.

"I know you already have your own church, and this would be a little bit more than services, I guess, but—"

"Joe." Lindsay spoke in the same warning tone she used when Emma tried to sneak a cookie before dinner.

"Now, just hear me out. You see, it's just that my friend Brett from the Brighton Post and his wife, Tricia, keep bugging me about coming to their church in Milford and then to lunch at their house. Their pestering is excruciating, believe me."

"Oh, I believe you," she answered in a tone that suggested she was at least smiling.

"Anyway, this time they broke me down. I told them I would go with them tomorrow under one condition."

He waited for her to bite, but she was quiet for so long that he worried she wouldn't even nibble.

"What condition?" she said flatly.

"That you and Emma would come with me."

"*We* were your condition?"

"With Brett and Tricia, the condition was that I be allowed to bring guests. A specific two to be exact."

"Are you saying that you'll only go if Emma and I go?"

"Of course not. That would mean I was using guilt to convince you, and that wouldn't be right." He smiled into the receiver. "But if you were to *volunteer,* then that would be different."

"Oh, that really *would* be different."

"So?" As he waited, her hesitation was telling. His disappointment was just as revealing.

Then she cleared her throat. "Joe Rossetti, Emma and I would very much like to escort you to church and then to lunch at your friends' house."

"I would be delighted to attend with you." But he didn't feel all that much *delight* over his victory. Now, *manipulative,* that was exactly how he felt.

Lindsay was the first to break into a chuckle, and he joined her, even if he had to force it.

"You missed your calling on the other end of the legal system," she said when she stopped. "You're good at persuasion. You should have been a defense attorney."

"Now I'll need to wash out my ears to get rid of that grimy thought. That's like suggesting that the Lone Ranger should pop down off Silver's back and join up with a gang of bank robbers."

She laughed out loud this time. "I wouldn't have thought it was that extreme."

"Believe me, it is."

"Joe."

Her small voice signaled that the time for levity was over. He braced himself. Was she going to back out now? He couldn't blame her. It was a cheap shot, using her concern about his faith to convince her to go somewhere with him, not to mention a big hint that he should be more concerned about his faith himself.

"Yeah."

"Have you asked yourself why you're trying so hard?"

"A couple of times."

"Did you give yourself any answers?"

"Not any good ones." Or answers he was prepared to share. And he refused to read anything into the fact that this would be the first time he'd brought a woman around his friends. He hoped Brett and Tricia had the good sense not to mention it to Lindsay.

"And Joe?" she said, as though she recognized that his thoughts had drifted. "Thanks for asking."

His pulse was pounding in his ears as he ended the call. What had just happened? Like the sand in an hourglass, its center slipping through the narrow gap and leaving the sides to collapse in upon themselves, something had shifted between them. He'd been the one helping her—at first to find answers and then to find her way.

But something had changed. Did Lindsay recognize it, too? He hadn't felt compelled to find some way to be with her because she needed him. It was because he needed her. Lindsay was proof positive that hope and faith could survive tragedy, that there would be tomorrows, even after the worst possible today. Then a thought crossed his mind that he'd never considered before: perhaps it was he who'd needed her all along.

The next morning, the benediction at Hickory Ridge Community Church had barely been spoken before a young couple with a whole brood of children hurried their way. Lindsay steadied herself, feeling as unsettled as she had since Joe picked her and Emma up that morning. Or, if she was being completely honest, since she'd hung up the phone the night before.

There were so many grinning faces that they blocked off the end of the pew. If Joe hadn't already told her that his friend had married a widow with three children, and the couple had two more together, Lindsay would have been surprised by the age span from teenager to toddler.

She wouldn't have had any trouble figuring out that the man was a police officer if she hadn't known that. His commanding presence and straight posture as he scooted down the pew gave him away. With a little blonde girl close to Emma's age propped on his right hip, Brett reached out to grip Joe's hand with his free left hand.

"Hey, buddy. We thought you were going to bail on us after all."

"We were just running a little late," Joe told him, pulling Emma up into his arms. "Anyway, have I ever bailed before?" As soon as his friend released his hand, he held it up as if to stop Brett's response. "Oh. Forget it. Don't answer that."

"Little ones definitely make it tougher to get out the door in the morning," Brett said.

Joe gestured to the children surrounding the woman at the end of the pew. "You and Tricia should know that better than anybody."

The simple image that struck Lindsay then—

of that large family greeting the small one she, Joe and Emma made—was so powerful that her breath caught. She turned away to retrieve her purse and Bible to cover her reaction. She couldn't allow herself to keep daydreaming about Joe.

Wasn't it enough that she'd been imagining his face all week on the ultrasound screen at work, though she hadn't seen him in person? One time, while she was performing an ultrasound for two excited parents-to-be, she'd even imagined herself as that expectant mother, with Joe cast in the role of the husband holding her hand.

Those were solid reasons she should have declined Joe's invitation last night. Reasons she'd ignored. She never would have been able to tell him no thank you, anyway. She'd fallen into the deep end of a pool, and it was becoming clear that she couldn't swim.

"I'm Brett Lancaster. You must be Lindsay."

She turned around to find Joe's friend extending his free left hand. After he shook her hand, he turned to the child.

"And you must be Emma. I've heard a lot about you."

Lindsay definitely couldn't say the same about Joe's friends. Everything she knew about the Lancasters, she'd learned during the ten-minute drive from Wixom to Milford.

Brett stepped back again to his family and gestured toward the petite brunette holding a toddler who looked just like her.

"Lindsay and Emma, this is my wife, Tricia, and that's our youngest, Claire, with her. Then we have Lani, Rusty Jr., Max and—" he paused and looked down at the preschooler in his arms "—this is Anna."

"There will be a test after lunch," Joe said.

"But we promise we'll let you cheat." Tricia assisted her with a warm smile. "I still don't know how you got Joe to come. He's been to our church exactly twice in the six years I've known him. One of those was our wedding, and he was obligated to come that time because he was the best man."

"Then I'm glad I could help out," Lindsay said.

She sneaked a look at Joe, but Brett caught her doing it and gave her a knowing grin. What did Joe's friend know that she didn't? And for that matter, she couldn't understand why it was important enough to Joe that she and Emma attend church with him that he'd ruined a good track record of turning down his friends' invitations.

She wanted to explain away his determination as the response of a guy who wasn't used to rejection, but that excuse didn't hold up any more than her explanation that she'd come today for Joe's spiritual well-being alone. That was her story, and she wanted to stick to it, but the pile of rejected outfits on her bed this morning and the butterflies flitting madly in her belly were making it difficult to hold her ground.

"Did you enjoy the service?" Tricia asked her, unaware that Lindsay had taken a hiatus from the conversation.

"Yes, it was really welcoming," Lindsay said. "And the 'Parable of the Talents' always makes for a good sermon."

Lindsay figured at least Reverend Bob Woods hadn't spoken on the Ten Commandments and mentioned that she should be honoring her mother and father because she would have been squirming in her seat over that one. She'd told her parents she and Emma would be visiting a new church closer to home, but she'd neglected to mention who would be joining her. If she really believed she was an adult who didn't have to report to her parents, then why was she being so secretive about it?

"I don't know about you, but I can't help relating to that last servant, burying his cash in the ground to keep it from disappearing." Tricia tilted her head to indicate her family. "Especially with all these guys around."

"I'll second that," Brett said.

Tricia started for the door with the others following closely behind her. She stopped and turned back to Lindsay.

"This is going to be fun," she said. "I'm sure all the kids will be friends by this afternoon."

"That sounds great, doesn't it, Emma?" Lindsay felt the same thing about herself with Tricia and Brett, and she couldn't help feeling excited over the prospect. Aside from Joe, they would be the first friends she'd made since she and Emma had become a family.

"Are we going to play?" Emma wanted to know.

"We sure are," the older daughter, whom Brett had introduced as Lani, told her.

As they stepped outside and started for their cars, Lindsay finally began to relax. She even smiled when Joe galloped toward the truck with Emma on his back, leaving the rest of them trailing behind.

Maybe coming today wasn't a mistake after all. Not only had she been there for Joe as he took a first baby step toward reclaiming his faith, but she would be able to give Emma and even herself the chance to make some new friends. Contrary to what her parents seemed to think, she knew she could make time for friends without losing her focus on Emma. That could apply to Joe, too, if she could forget her ridiculous fantasies about him.

The older Lancaster children guided their younger siblings to the family Suburban, while Brett and Tricia walked with Lindsay to the truck.

Joe already had turned on the engine and blasted the air-conditioning and was buckling Emma into her child safety seat in the truck's second-row bench when they caught up with him.

"Hey, Joe," Brett said. "I just realized something."

Slowly, Joe turned back to face them, leaving the door open to let out the steamy air. "Are you sure it's something you need to share with the rest of us?"

"Oh, I'm sure," Brett said.

Lindsay looked back and forth between them, not understanding, but Brett's grin and Joe's frown hinted that one of them wouldn't be thrilled to hear what the other had to say.

"Then what did you realize?" Joe said in a flat tone.

"That this is first time you've ever brought a woman over to meet us."

Tricia turned to her husband, her eyes wide. "You're absolutely right." But then she grinned, as if she'd been part of the plan to tease him all along.

It was all Lindsay could do to catch a breath as her rationalizations concerning Joe disappeared faster than the cars pulling from the church lot. Was this really a "meet the friends" event for Joe, rather than simply a long-overdue visit to church?

Okay, she was the first woman he'd brought to meet them, but was that significant?

Joe's expression was so difficult to read that Lindsay couldn't decide whether he was angry or embarrassed or something else entirely. He seemed to have lost the confidence that he usually wore, even out of uniform. As his gaze connected with hers, he chewed his bottom lip, but then he shrugged.

"You see what happens when people get married?" Joe shook his head. "All that bliss turns their brains to mush, and then they can't help projecting their happy status onto everyone around them."

"Now, that's an interesting theory, but I wonder why you would jump to that conclusion in this instance," Brett said. "I had been just about to say how nice it was that you finally brought a friend along." He leaned toward Lindsay conspiratorially. "After all these years, his stories are getting old."

"Sorry my friendship has been such a chore for you."

Brett and Tricia looked at each other and burst out laughing. Joe frowned at the two of them, but soon he was laughing, too. Lindsay smiled, though she wasn't sure what had just happened. It must have been an inside joke, the kind shared by close friends…or sisters who just happened to be best friends.

At the thought, Lindsay straightened, expecting the relentless fist that always gripped her heart when she thought of Delia. This time, though, the squeeze wasn't as tight, and she was even able to smile a little over those private jokes she once shared with her sister.

Sure, remembering hurt now, and probably always would to some degree, but she didn't want to lose all of those precious memories that would allow a little girl to know the mother who left this world too soon. It was strange how being with these people who never knew her sister made her feel closer to Delia's memory.

"Well, Joe, it looks like you're already boring her, too." Brett patted his friend on the shoulder. "That's not a good sign."

"Guess I am in trouble."

"What?" Lindsay shook her head. "That's not what I— I didn't mean…"

But they laughed again, and she let it go at that. Joe lifted an eyebrow, as if he wondered what she'd been thinking about, but he didn't press.

"Aunt Lindsay," Emma called from inside the truck. "Can we go now?"

"That's a good idea," Tricia said, as she glanced at the Suburban, with all its windows open and children hanging their heads out of them, as if they were smothering inside. "If we don't get back to the house soon, there's going to be an uprising."

When she and Joe climbed into the truck, she expected questions, but he must have been preparing himself for the same thing from her because he didn't ask any as they followed the Lancasters to their new house. It was probably a good idea that they didn't talk. If he started asking her questions, she might have to admit a few things she wasn't ready to say, even to herself.

Chapter Eleven

"He's a great guy, isn't he?"

Lindsay started at the sound of Tricia's voice and adjusted her cane to regain balance. She'd thought she was alone as she moved about the Lancasters' study, staring at framed documents and shadow boxes with souvenirs of a life dedicated to public service. But now she'd been caught red-handed, searching for a familiar face in the photos.

She turned to find the young mother standing in the doorway watching her. "You mean Brett?" she asked, managing to keep a straight face.

"We both know who I meant." Tricia smiled. "But my husband's not half-bad, either."

"I'm sure he would appreciate hearing that," Lindsay said with a chuckle.

"Wouldn't want to make him overconfident or anything."

"You probably boosted his self-esteem irreversibly when you agreed to marry him."

"Remind me to tell Joe that we're keeping you. We knew you had to be special if he brought you here."

"He's never introduced you to any of his female friends?"

"I guess he couldn't choose which one," Tricia said. "At least with girlfriends, he never kept any of them around long enough to make dinner plans."

"Oh." She was having a hard time reconciling the man she was hearing about with the one she'd come to know. The one who'd stepped up to help her and her niece. The one who'd carried her away from the accident scene in his arms.

Tricia watched her for several seconds. "Don't be too disappointed in him. It was a long time ago. It just takes some of us longer than others to find our way."

Lindsay knew what that was like, but it was strange, realizing that the man who'd helped her had his own issues. She'd known about the loss of his mother, so it shouldn't have surprised her that he'd had problems with women.

"He's really been a good friend to Emma and me," she said, feeling as if she should come to his defense.

"Yes, Joe's very attached…to Emma," Tricia said.

Lindsay had been taking in the basketball-team

pictures and the Thin Blue Line charity certificates, but she looked back to Tricia now, sensing her unspoken message.

"I don't know what we would have done without—wait." She jerked her head to look out the window. "Is Emma okay? You said she would be all right for a few minutes with—"

"Don't worry, Lindsay. She's fine. She's still playing out back with the kids. Lani and Rusty have everything under control with their new little mascot."

"Where are Brett and Joe?"

"In the garage, looking at Brett's new table saw. What is it about men and table saws? Yes, they're tables and they cut things, but beyond that, I don't get it."

They both laughed.

"Look at this place." Tricia reached out to touch an ancient state trooper's hat hanging on the wall. "We don't call it an office. It's our 'State Police Room.' Most of the members on the force have one in their homes."

"It looks like Brett has had a celebrated career."

Tricia brushed her hand over a portrait of her husband in uniform. "If you really want to see a tribute to heroism, you should see the room at Joe's dad's house. With Joe's father and grandfather living there together now, that place is like the state police Smithsonian."

"Joe told me he has big shoes to fill." Like her, did he sometimes wonder if he would ever measure up?

"You have no idea," Tricia said. "But he's doing a better job than he realizes of filling those shoes. Did you know that Brett and Joe used to be partners on midnights?"

Tricia waited for Lindsay's nod before she continued. "There's nobody Brett trusts more to have covering his back. Nobody I trust more to help keep my husband safe."

A lump formed in Lindsay's throat as she stared at a photo of Brett and Joe with their arms draped over each other's shoulders. True friends through thick and thin. Her relationship with Delia had been like that, with the added benefit of being sisters, as well.

"Joe told me about your accident," Tricia said in a quiet voice. "I'm so sorry for your loss. For you and Emma. I know what that kind of mind-numbing loss is like. So, if you ever need someone to talk to, someone who gets it..."

Lindsay nodded, and the woman who she'd met that day hugged her like a childhood friend. Joe had given her such a blessing by introducing her to these people.

Tricia pulled back from her and stared into Lindsay's eyes. "Joe has really struggled with guilt over being unable to save both you and your sister. He told Brett he played the scenario over and over, looking for what he could have done differently."

"He did everything he could," Lindsay said, finding that she really believed that, even if part of her still wondered if he'd helped the right victim first. "He was a hero."

"He doesn't he see it that way. It had to mean so much to him that you've forgiven him. That you've accepted him as a friend."

Had she forgiven him completely? Lindsay wasn't convinced. She hoped so because he deserved her forgiveness. He'd never deserved her blame, though she hadn't been ready to acknowledge that before.

"But then it's already a sign that you're a good person that your sister entrusted you with Emma's care."

"Thanks."

Tricia must have believed they'd spent enough time on that heavy topic because she turned back to Lindsay smiling.

"I still wonder how you convinced him to go to church with you. We've invited him so many times. He accepts our dinner invitations. He's a single guy, after all. But he's always amazingly busy on Sunday mornings."

"He told me he lost his faith after his mom died."

Tricia pointed to another picture of Brett and

Joe standing arm-in-arm. "Oh, Joe still believes. He's just not ready to admit it."

"I told him almost the same thing."

"Great minds think alike," Tricia said. "Good thing for Joe that our God is patient."

"That's a good thing for all of us."

The poem. It was a symbol that they were both right about Joe and his faith. Lindsay was tempted to tell Tricia about how he'd given her the poem about God the night of the accident, but she doubted that Joe would appreciate her sharing the story. He was embarrassed enough every time she mentioned it. She decided it was a story best left between the two of them.

"Are you ladies finished gabbing about us in here?"

Both turned to find Brett standing in the doorway where Tricia had been earlier. Since it was impossible to tell how long he'd been there, or if Joe was nearby, Lindsay was relieved she hadn't mentioned the poem.

"We have five—make that six—starving youngsters out there, and we've got Rossetti manning the grill, so I figured a call for backup might be in order."

"Uh-oh, we'd better get out there." Tricia linked arms with Lindsay and started for the door. As she passed her husband, she asked, "Is the fire department on standby?"

"No, but good call."

They were already out the back door by the time Brett caught up to them. He stepped closer to his wife, putting his arm around her and giving her a squeeze. "Did Lindsay pass the test…because if you're still not sure, I can make a quick call and come up with a lie detector…"

"She passed. We're keeping her. But you'd better let Rossetti know that his spot around here isn't as secure."

Lindsay followed them out into the huge fenced backyard, catching a glimpse of Joe, who looked like he had the grill more under control than Brett had suggested. The children were still playing on the wooden fort, so it didn't look as if any of them had passed out from starvation yet.

When Joe glanced up from the grill and smiled at Lindsay, her heart skipped a beat. No matter how Joe felt about her, she could no longer deny that her feelings for him went way beyond friendship.

During their visit, she'd learned a lot more about him. No, he wasn't perfect, but learning about his imperfections had only balanced the qualities she already knew he possessed—strength, dedication and empathy. His incongruities only made her more curious about him. The man with a spotted record with women, who'd been only kind to her. The brave police officer who was afraid to fail.

Her intense curiosity about him was just another signal that she was in too deep. Stepping away would be in her best interest. Her parents certainly believed that it was in Emma's best interest, but Lindsay knew now she wouldn't do it and not only because she disagreed with them. The need to know everything about Joe Rossetti and the need to be near him were too strong. Both of those things were so appealing, and yet they scared her to death.

The last strip of orange and magenta was clinging to the edge of the horizon when Joe sat down next to Lindsay on the front porch step of her condo. She shifted farther over, probably without realizing she was doing it, and glanced up the street. He didn't have to ask her for whom she was watching.

"Is she asleep?"

He nodded. "I only made it to the second page of *The Velveteen Rabbit*. Those Lancaster kids wore her out."

"She had a great time." She cleared her throat and didn't look his way as she added, "So did I."

"The kids thought Emma was great. She has a lot in common with the three older ones." He didn't have to say that he, too, shared the loss of a parent in common with all of them.

"She adored them, too."

Joe looked up in time to see that orange strip of sky disappear as if someone had colored it with a navy felt-tip pen. "You're probably wondering why a great couple like Brett and Tricia would ever be friends with a guy like me."

"I didn't wonder that. Brett said he was obligated since he was your first partner."

"Thanks." He reached over the space that separated them and poked her arm. "But it's true enough."

As he watched her under the yellow cast of the porch light, he had a hard time sensing her mood. Was she sorry she hadn't stuck to her guns and continued to avoid him, or was she just worried that her parents would pop in for a visit and decide that her spending time with him was some symbol that she was ignoring Emma?

"You're probably wondering why I had never brought a woman to meet my friends before. And why Brett made a big production of letting you know it."

"Well…"

"Oh. Tricia told you." He hated for Lindsay to know what a creep he'd been. "I wasn't such a great guy. I didn't treat women very well."

"Tricia just said you liked to date around."

"And if I know Tricia at all, then she didn't say it as pleasantly as that. I did once tell her husband that there were plenty of fish in the sea and there was no use reeling the same one in all the time."

Her lips lifted at that. "Okay, maybe she didn't say it harshly enough."

"I deserved that. I wasn't just dating around. I was avoiding relationships. What Tricia doesn't know—I never even got around to telling Brett about it—was why."

Lindsay gave him a dubious look that suggested there was no good reason to ever have treated women badly, and she was right, but he decided to tell her anyway.

"I got burned," he began, but had to take another breath before he could continue. "Her name was Chelsea. I was crazy about her."

Her eyes widened with questions, but she didn't ask.

"I had just taken my entrance exam for the third time. And failed again." He had to force himself to look up at her again. "Did I tell you I had to test four times before I finally was admitted to the Michigan State Police Recruit School? Not a proud time for a third-generation guy."

"No, you didn't tell me."

"Well, I had expected to pass that time and had planned to propose to her right afterward. Instead, I missed the mark again, and then Chelsea announced that she was dumping me for some other guy. Apparently, I'd been too focused on studying for the test and not enough on her."

He glanced over at Lindsay then, and the compassion in her eyes hurt almost more than the original breakup.

"Not only had I failed at the family business, now I had also failed at building the other thing the Rossetti men were known for. Blissful marriages. Dad and Grandpa adored Mom and Grandma and never got over their deaths. Even my brother, David, and his wife have been sickeningly happy."

"It's easy to see why you avoided relationships," she told him. "Why didn't you ever tell Brett this story?"

"Because Brett got dumped himself by his first fiancée. I was supposed to be his best man in that first wedding, too." He glanced over at her, surprised to find her studying him so intently. "Anyway, his story was more pitiful than mine, so I didn't want to compete."

"And you didn't want to share your humiliation."

"That, too." He grinned. There was no getting anything past Lindsay Collins.

Lindsay had moved closer to him. He hated that she might have shifted out of pity, but his nerve endings came alive with her nearness, and her light floral perfume invaded his senses. He could feel her gaze on him. She was trying to figure him out, struggling.

"So, if this dating around thing was working for you, then why did you stop?"

"It stopped being fun…if it ever was. And after a while, I realized it wasn't any of the other women's faults that I got dumped." He smiled out into the near darkness and then added, "Also, I decided that my mom would have been disappointed to know that after all of her work to raise David and me to be gentlemen, I'd grown up to treat women with anything less than respect."

"For someone who's been gone for well over two decades, she still has a lot of impact on you."

"I'll take that as a compliment."

She turned and smiled at him then. "You should."

For the next few minutes, the only sounds around them were the rumble of passing cars, the persistent chirps of crickets and the battling television voices in other condo units. Had telling the whole story made him look better or worse to Lindsay? He didn't even bother asking himself why he cared so much. He did, and that was all there was to it.

"Why are you telling me all of this?" she said.

"You mean besides that fact that I don't want you to see me for the scum I really was?"

"Besides that."

"And besides that you're especially easy to talk to."

"Now, I know it has to be more than that." She laughed. "No one ever accused me of being easy to talk to."

"I don't know."

How could he explain his temptation to open up to her from that first day at the park, when sharing like that had always been a foreign language to him? How could he explain his need to confide secrets in her like an adolescent girl at a slumber party? He'd never felt the need to share with Chelsea, and he'd thought he loved her. Now he wasn't sure he'd ever known what love was.

"I guess if we're sharing, you probably want me to tell you some story from my dark dating history?"

As a matter of fact, he didn't want her to, but he couldn't tell her that. Then he would have to explain how the hair at his nape bristled at the thought of any man who'd had the privilege of holding her or touching her face. How could he be jealous over a woman he'd insisted was only a friend? He couldn't, but he wasn't ready to admit any of that to her, either.

"If you want," he said finally.

"Well, that's the funny part," she said, but there

was no humor in her voice. "The truth is, I don't have a dating history." She cleared her throat. "I haven't. Ever."

"Never ever?" He didn't mean to look at her as if she'd grown a second head, but he must have because she stared down at her hands.

"I never intended for it to be that way. It just... was." She didn't look up at him as she continued to speak. "You get used it after a while. The invisibility. If not that, the looks that said while they would be more than happy to borrow my chemistry notes, they had no interest taking me out for coffee. Men just never noticed me that way."

"Someone as amazing as you? How is that even possible?"

Joe wasn't sure whether he'd spoken those words aloud or in the safety of his thoughts until Lindsay stared back at him, a deer-in-the-headlights look in her eyes. Her mouth was slack, and he found himself studying her lips, those same full red lips he'd noticed that first day in the squad room and had been trying to ignore ever since.

If she hadn't dated, had those lips never been kissed, as well? She hadn't said that, but the possibility was there that her mouth may never have been properly adored by someone who'd taken the time to notice even that fine line in the center of her bottom lip. Suddenly, he wanted more than anything to be that first man to kiss Lindsay Collins. The only.

As if she'd become gravity and he just a piece of rock caught in its magnetic pull, she drew him to her, without her knowledge, and from that shielded look, maybe without the certainty that she wanted it to happen. He leaned toward her in a move he'd practiced with dozens of forgettable faces. But as he drew close, staring into those wide eyes, he felt as if he was about to have his very first kiss, too.

A shriek coming from inside the house stopped him, his face mere inches from hers. Lindsay might have been frozen in place only a moment before, but at the sound of her niece's voice, she was up and rushing for the door. She threw open the storm door and ran for the stairs, taking them by twos. Joe was right at her heels.

"I'm coming, Emma," she called out.

The door to the child's room was open only a crack, but Lindsay pushed it wide and hurried inside. Emma sat rocking in the middle of the bed with knees drawn up to her chest, her arms wrapped around them.

Lindsay sat on the edge of the bed. "What is it honey? Another bad dream?"

"I miss my mommy," Emma moaned, not answering the question, or maybe answering one her aunt hadn't asked.

"I know you do, sweetheart." In a quiet voice, she added, "I miss her, too."

The child looked up at Lindsay with twin tears trailing down her cheeks. Joe continued to watch the heartbreaking scene from the doorway, wanting to step in but realizing it wasn't his place. This was Lindsay's responsibility, and she was handling it flawlessly.

"It's going to be okay, Emma," she crooned. "*We're* going to be okay. You and me."

So different from the first night when she'd called him in a panic, Lindsay was calm as she inched closer to Emma until she was right next to her. Then she gently rubbed the child's back in tiny circles.

Soon she was cradling Emma in a scene so precious that Joe's heart ached just watching. He'd spent a lifetime trying not to become involved, and right now there was nothing he wanted more than to get wrapped up in this situation and in this little family.

After several minutes of rocking and soothing, Lindsay seemed to remember that he was still there and turned her head to look at him in the doorway. She smiled. No awkward moment about the near miss of a kiss from a few minutes before, she seemed to have forgotten it altogether.

"If you want me to, I can stay until she's back to sleep," he said, in a low voice.

Lindsay shook her head. "That's all right. Emma needs me. I'm just going to stay with her for a while until she gets back to sleep." As if she expected him to argue, she smiled. "We'll be fine."

"I'll check in with you later, then." He backed out of the room, pulling the door closed behind him.

He wanted Lindsay to be confident and capable when caring for Emma. That was his whole goal for spending time with her, right? So why did he hate feeling so extraneous now?

He grabbed his shoes that he'd left in the entry, went outside and pulled the door closed, checking the doorknob behind him to ensure it was locked. He was a police officer, after all. He might be going home, but he wouldn't leave Lindsay and Emma vulnerable when he left.

Vulnerability. That had to be it. He'd opened himself up to Lindsay in a way he never had to anyone. He'd even told her about the humiliation over Chelsea, a story he'd planned to take with him to the grave. After all of that, Lindsay had all but shoved him out the door. To be fair, she'd had a little on her mind at the time, but the dismissal hurt just the same.

He couldn't be vulnerable. Not at work, not in any relationship, and Lindsay made him feel utterly unprotected in both of those ways. He'd promised himself he wouldn't go in too deep, wouldn't risk more than he was prepared to lose, and here he was setting himself up for heartbreak.

He managed to make it all the way to his truck before thoughts of that almost-kiss whacked him like a .45-caliber round to a chest protected by a bulletproof vest—no blood but a world of ache. It would have been a mistake for him to kiss her, but even now as he imagined her sweet smile and trusting eyes, he wanted to repeat the moment again with a more perfect ending.

What had he been thinking? He'd told himself he needed to keep his distance from Lindsay, and yet he'd been drawn to her like a moth to a pretty, bright light. Even when she'd been the sensible one and had tried to put space between them, he'd used attending church, of all things, to change her mind.

Just because Joe couldn't bear not being able to see her smile or to hear her laugh or smell the scent of her hair, that didn't mean he should have manipulated her into spending more time with him. The God he'd kept at arm's length would probably not look kindly on that.

Joe grumbled as he gripped the steering wheel and pulled away from her curb. He didn't know her thoughts about what had taken place tonight, but she deserved an explanation for his behavior. She deserved to know why, despite all of his efforts to pursue her, that the two of them couldn't be together for their own good. So why did he get the feeling that he would be the one with the broken heart?

Chapter Twelve

Lindsay's eyes shot open, and she jerked her head up, looking around and trying to get her bearings in the darkness. Where was she? But the familiar slowly came into view, the long, mirrored bureau from her childhood bedroom, her grandmother's old rocker in the corner.

It was only a bad dream, like Emma's from last night.

Dropping her head to the pillow, Lindsay shifted at the feel of her damp hair against her neck. She glanced at the digital clock that provided the room's only light. The numbers flashed 3:00.

"Lord, please give me comfort," she whispered and then slowly released her grip on the coverlet.

She took a deep breath and waited. Usually, her dreams disappeared from her memory before she could replay them after she awakened, but this time was different. The images from her nightmare had come with her into consciousness, their lights blinding, their sounds piercing.

Turning on her side, she flipped on the lamp on her bedside table, hoping her thoughts would clear, but she could still hear the screams, Delia's and her own, and she could still see the car spinning out of control. From there it was like a computer slideshow played on high speed, with flashes of Delia slumped in the seat next to her, rain pelting the cracked windshield, a shocking circle of light from outside the window.

Lindsay squeezed her eyes closed. Strange how she'd thought she wanted to remember, and yet now all she wanted to do was to close off these memories and let them continue to hide beyond the dark barrier of her subconscious. Opening her eyes again, she focused on that rocking chair, its presence a calm surety in a world that otherwise had the unsettled foundation of a fault line.

Pushing that stringy wet hair back from her face, she shook her head. Was she really getting her memory back, or were these just images her mind had manufactured from the information printed in the police report, or even the enhanced details that Joe had given her?

As a test, she closed her eyes and reached back into the recesses of her thoughts, searching for more. Nothing. Her eyes fluttered open, and she couldn't decide whether to be frustrated or re-lieved, but she still didn't know whether or not the memories were real. Whether there would be more or if any of those would be authentic, she couldn't begin to know.

"Why now?" she whispered into the room, il-luminated in the center by the lamp, but still dark and shadowy in the corners. After all of the time she'd been searching for answers, it didn't make sense that her own mind would choose that night to start putting the puzzle pieces together while she slept.

Then it became clear. Joe had almost kissed her last night. Or at least that was what she thought had been about to happen. She'd always heard that a kiss could change everything, and she'd had no personal experience to know whether or not it was true. She still didn't, but she couldn't help wonder-ing if an almost-kiss could have the same impact of upending a person's equilibrium. It seemed to have done that to hers.

Last night, she'd held her breath and waited and waited as he'd paused, his mouth only inches from hers. But then Emma had cried out, offer-ing Lindsay an escape. Sure, she'd run, mostly because she wanted to be there for the child who was now the center of her life, but a small part of her was also panicking in the intensity of that moment. A novice's mistake, right?

Hadn't she wanted him to kiss her? She smiled at that. The question should have been how much. She'd probably wanted him to kiss her since that first time he'd shown up at her condo like the cavalry, ready to save her from that crazy afternoon. Okay, not then. She'd been annoyed with him then. But soon after that and pretty much constantly ever since.

Then why had she sent him away last night when she'd wanted to be near him, when she'd wanted so much for him to comfort *her* as she'd comforted Emma? Because she had to. She'd needed to prove to herself that she could handle a difficult situation with her niece without calling Joe, without calling anyone for help.

She'd also needed to make it clear in her mind that she wanted to be near Joe, not because she needed a support system to help her with Emma but because he just might be the man God had planned for her. She was determined to find out for sure. She'd done what she needed to do, and now she knew what she wanted.

Did he know now, as well? Was he sure that he wanted to be with her?

It still amazed her that Joe had opened up to her as much as he had last night. She was surprised that he'd told her about the woman who'd hurt him when he hadn't shared that story with anyone else, but it shocked her more that any woman who'd been blessed enough to have Joe's heart wouldn't have recognized the gift it was.

She supposed she shouldn't have been surprised that he'd shared that secret with her when he'd opened to her a few times before in a way he probably didn't with anyone else. She didn't know what she'd done to deserve to be his confidante, but she was honored by his trust.

They hadn't made any more plans for today, but she had the afternoon off, and she hoped Joe would call her so they could get together later in the day. Maybe he would even try to kiss her again today, and if he did, this time she would let him.

Lindsay sat up and fluffed her pillow and then leaned over to the table and switched off the lamp. Darkness covered the room again, but it was peaceful now, the quiet inviting. Pulling the coverlet up, she settled it just beneath her chin and closed her eyes. She looked forward to her dreams now because she just knew they would be sweet ones, where she could be found safe in Joe's arms.

Joe's legs felt as if they were weighted with chains as he climbed from his patrol car, parked down the street from Lindsay's condo, and started down the sidewalk. That she'd seemed so pleased when he'd asked if he could pop by on his lunch hour, even mentioning that she had news to share, made him dread what he had to say more than he already had. But the incident at the post overnight had convinced him even more that it had to be said.

How was he supposed to explain backing away from her when he'd been so insistent on getting involved in her life, continually justifying his need to spend time with her? *Oh, my bad, I've just been giving you the wrong message for weeks.*

He didn't know whom he was trying to kid anyway. Even when he'd called her this morning, his heart had tripped incriminatingly. She deserved an explanation for his behavior last night, though, and if he could come up with one, he would give it to her.

A car had been parked in the way, so he hadn't seen them at first, but as Joe walked down the sidewalk toward her condo, he caught sight of Emma and Lindsay on the postage stamp of a front yard. Emma splashed merrily in a wading pool, and Lindsay sat in a lawn chair next to the pool, with her toes dipping in the water.

The scene was so sweet that Joe's heart squeezed as he stopped to watch them. Lindsay looked so young and pretty, with her hair tied up in a loose bun with tresses escaping to flutter across her cheek. She'd probably only been planning to cool off by getting her feet wet, but she'd gotten more than she'd bargained for, if her damp, pink T-shirt and tan shorts were any indication.

His throat filled with emotion as he realized he'd never wanted anything as much as he wanted to be a part of the picture that the two of them made, and not for just one day, either. Joe was a man warring between duty and his heart's desire. He knew which one had to win, but that didn't make it hurt any less.

After a big splash, Lindsay laughed and reached down to tug on one of Emma's ponytails. They looked so happy together, just the two of them, that Joe wondered whether he should approach at all. If there had been a time when Lindsay wasn't completely natural with children, that time had long since passed.

He hated to interrupt such a perfect moment when what he had to say could just as easily have been said on the phone. It was the coward's way out, and he knew it, but a good trooper knew not to go into an uncertain situation without backup. He had none. But just as he started back toward the car, Lindsay looked his way. She smiled when she saw him.

"Oh, Joe. You're here. Pull up a chair. I left one over there for you. The water's fine."

"Thanks. But we send out our uniforms when we want them washed." He grabbed the extra lawn chair that she'd set next to the front porch steps, but he set it up a few feet back from the swimming pool. He took off his hat and balanced it on his knee.

Lindsay smiled as she dragged her own chair back to his and sat down, brushing at the damp sleeve of her T-shirt. "What? That's got to be unheard of, a single guy turning down free laundry services."

"I try to be an original."

Emma had been crouching down, trying to blow bubbles on the water's surface, but she popped up as if she only now realized that he was there.

"Trooper Joe. Look at me. I'm swimming."

"You sure are. You're getting Aunt Lindsay wet, too."

The child grinned over at him. "She likes it."

"I think she would like doing anything, as long as it's with you."

Emma grabbed her net bag of toys set outside the rim of the pool and dumped them all in the water. Instead of playing with those toys floating around her, though, she leaned forward and dunked her face in the water.

She shot up and wiped her eyes. "See, Aunt Lindsay, I can go underwater."

"You sure can. That's really big."

Joe couldn't help grinning at Emma as he remembered the first few times he'd shared with the two of them, and the child had clearly favored him. He was pleased that Emma had learned to value her aunt.

"She's really adapted well, hasn't she?"

But when he turned to Lindsay, he found her watching him instead of her niece. The blush he knew so well dotted her cheeks, and she looked away just as she had when he'd first met her. He couldn't blame her. He'd changed the rules last night, and now she couldn't know what to expect from him. She would expect what he needed to tell her least of all.

As if she'd taken control of her embarrassment, Lindsay turned back to him. "You said things were crazy at the post today. What happened?"

"What didn't?"

But she only looked at him, as if she wasn't buying his attempt to make light of what had happened.

"Well, for one thing, Trooper Garrett Taylor nearly got himself shot on Interstate 96."

At the ashen look that appeared on Lindsay's face, he was sorry that he'd phrased the comment that way. She might have been seven months past her own tragedy, but the accident on that same interstate was probably never far from her thoughts.

"How awful," she said, after a long pause. "But he's okay, right?"

"Yeah. Because of some quick thinking, he got lucky."

"Oh. Praise God for that."

Though he might have a few weeks before, he didn't argue with her. He didn't care if it was God or just great reflexes, but his friend was alive, and he was grateful.

"What happened? Can you tell me?"

Joe shrugged. "It's a matter of public record now that the report is filed, anyway. It might even make the six o'clock news if it's a slow news day and nothing bloodier or more sensational shows up before then."

She glanced to see if Emma had been listening and then looked back to him again. "Well, tell me."

"It's a risk that troopers take the moment they approach vehicles to check licenses and registrations or to hand out citations." He waited for her to guess, but when she didn't, he added, "That the driver will pull a gun."

Lindsay shivered visibly. "That's what happened today?"

Joe nodded. "We all like to think we're prepared for it, but all it takes is one distracted moment."

Lindsay drew her eyebrows together as she studied him. "Are you saying that Trooper Taylor was distracted, and that's how he almost got shot?"

"Well, that's how he says it happened. He said

when the suspect pulled a weapon, he was a second too late in drawing his own weapon. In a situation like this one, you're either on your game or not. Just like that—" Joe snapped his fingers "—and any one of us could be dead."

"But that's not what happened this time."

"No. That's why I said Garrett was lucky. The suspect couldn't manage to get a shot off and drive away at the same time. The shot went wide."

"Was he able to get the shooter?"

"This time that turned out okay, too," he said with a shrug. "He radioed in the plate number and then joined the chase. The suspect was apprehended near the Howell exit."

Lindsay seemed to mull over what he'd said as she watched Emma flopping in the water. Finally, she turned back to him.

"Okay, Joe. I get it that you're trying to give me some deep message with this story, but somehow I'm missing it. Yes, it could have been bad had the suspect's shot been on target. It could have been devastating. But it wasn't."

He sighed, deciding to spell it out for her. "Devastating is exactly how it *would* have been if I'd been the one on patrol, if I'd been the one to approach that driver. If it had been me, you would be watching my obituary on the six o'clock news."

Lindsay just stared at him, her eyes wide and

too bright. "Why…why would you say something like that?"

"I'm sorry. But I just wanted you to know…I wanted to explain. My judgment is off on the job, and I used to trust it implicitly. My edge…" he paused and plunged forward "…is just gone. I'm a liability every time I'm out on the roadways. I'm afraid every time I'm out there that I'm going to mess up again and someone's going to get hurt."

He hadn't intended to include the word *again* in that comment, but it came out against his will.

Lindsay balanced her elbow on her leg and held her chin between her thumb and forefinger. "How long have you been feeling this way?"

"Ever since," he began, and then had to start over. "Ever since—"

"Since the day when you pulled one sister from the wreckage of a car accident and her other sister died," she completed for him. She didn't pose it as a question.

"I've questioned myself every day on the job since then." He squeezed his eyes shut, pinching the bridge of his nose. "I should have—I don't know—maybe if I'd…"

He let his words trail away because even now he couldn't name a single thing he would have done differently if he'd come upon an identical accident today and the victims had presented in the same manner.

"I'm done swimming now."

Joe startled at the sound of Emma's voice, and he was surprised to see her standing right in front of them. When had she jumped out of the water? When had Lindsay wrapped her in that fluffy beach towel? At least Lindsay had been paying attention to her while she swam.

"Can I watch a movie now?" Emma asked her aunt.

"Okay, but just for a little while."

When Lindsay stood, he started to stand as well, but she indicated for him to remain seated. "I'll get her into some dry clothes and situated, and then I'll be right back."

He watched after her as Lindsay let Emma pull her by the hand into the house. It took him a few seconds to realize she wasn't using her cane. While he waited for Lindsay to return, he sifted through the rest of the things he should tell her— those final details from the accident and why his lost confidence signaled that he shouldn't have tried to get close to her. She deserved to know all of it.

But when she stepped outside again, closing only the storm door so she could still see into the living room, and he joined her on the steps as she'd indicated, all of those things he should have said flitted away. Instead, he found himself blurting the question that had been plaguing him for weeks.

"How can I ever be sure that a decision I make won't hurt someone else or get someone else killed?"

For a long time Lindsay didn't say anything. She must have been waiting for him to look at her because when he finally did, she was watching him, her face heartbreakingly compassionate.

"I'm sorry, but you can't."

Chapter Thirteen

Lindsay's heart squeezed as Joe leaned forward on the step next to her, bracing his elbows on his knees and holding his head in his hands. Her throat burned with the words she'd just spoken, the words that must have placed more weight on Joe's shoulders than he could bear.

Why hadn't she noticed all of this before? The worry lines that had formed on his forehead, the loss of that strict posture he always carried in uniform. She could have excused herself by saying that she had no history of Joe before the accident for comparison, but even she had to recognize that his feelings about that night went beyond simple guilt. He blamed himself for her sister's death.

She'd been so selfish to press him for answers about the accident when he felt that way. In all the time he'd spent with Emma and her, through all of the feelings she'd developed for him, she hadn't been sensitive enough to give him the absolution he craved.

Even today, she'd only been thinking about herself and that almost-kiss from last night. An event she just might have imagined. Well, her selfishness stopped now. He deserved a break, and she was going to give it to him.

"What happened the night of the accident wasn't your fault," she told him. "You did the best you could. We both wish you would have been able to pull Delia out, too, but it wasn't meant to be."

He shook his head. "But I could have—"

"You did everything you could. Everything," she insisted. "More than most people would have done. Like at the hospital...after."

His laugh bore no real humor. "You know we're not supposed to get involved with victims like that."

"Maybe not, but I appreciated that you did."

Though he'd become a lot more involved with her since that first night at the hospital, neither of them mentioned it. Still, the truth of it hung heavily in the silence between them.

He lifted one shoulder and lowered it, but it was obvious that he either wasn't accepting anything she'd said or that her words only upset him more. From the strange way he was acting today, pulling away from her, she wasn't sure she would have many more opportunities to tell him, so she wanted to do it now.

"You have to stop blaming yourself." She waited until he looked over at her to add, "I don't blame you."

"You don't?"

The skepticism in his eyes seemed to battle with belief, and even though she wasn't certain that she meant it in the deepest part of her heart, she wanted nothing more than to remove his questions. "No, I don't."

"Thanks." He paused, as if considering what she'd said, before continuing. "I wish I could say the same."

"Don't you think it's a little narcissistic to believe you wield that much power or control?"

Joe blinked, signaling she'd surprised him as she'd hoped she would. He watched her with his side vision, his lips lifting.

"If you're trying to make me feel better, you might want to try a different approach."

"All I'm saying is that unless you can take full credit for every life you help to save, then you can't take full responsibility when things don't go your way." She held up her hand before he could provide some witty comeback. "And in case you haven't figured this one out yet, you *can't* take full credit because you're not in control. God is in control."

She waited, expecting an argument from him, but he only nodded.

"I know I can't."

"Trooper Rossetti, sometimes you surprise me. If you understand that, then why are you wasting so much time worrying about what can go wrong?"

"I can't help it," he said with a shrug. "I'm not in a field where I can backspace over my mistakes. Mine get zipped up in plastic and sent off to the morgue."

His words were uncomfortably blunt, inspiring scenes that she still couldn't produce from memory, but she wouldn't allow herself to be sidetracked by the thought. Joe needed her support this time, and she was determined to give it to him.

"Listen. You can't buy trouble like that, waiting for the worst. Don't you remember, in Matthew 6:34, that Jesus says, 'Therefore, do not be anxious about tomorrow, for tomorrow will be anxious for itself. Let the day's own trouble be sufficient for the day.'"

It was Joe's turn to grin. "Did you know that one off the top of your head, or did you memorize it just for me?"

She elbowed him. "I knew it, but it sounds like one you should memorize, too."

"I'll try."

Lindsay turned to check on Emma through the window, but when she shifted back she found him watching her. Like always, her skin warmed and she just seemed to awaken under his steady gaze.

"What are you looking at?"

"An amazing woman. You might know her. She's the one who always surprises *me* with her insights. The one who helps me get my head on straight."

Her cheeks burned over his compliment, and she didn't know what to do with her hands, so she gripped them in her lap. Something had changed between them in the past few minutes, something that felt monumental, and all she could do was to sit there and wait for whatever he planned to tell her.

"Did you know that I came over here today to tell you I couldn't see you anymore because you remind me of the accident where I made my biggest mistake?"

Lindsay swallowed as disappointment buried hope under a pile of rubble. It only made sense that Joe would feel that way because he reminded her of her darkest day as well. *She* could get past that, but maybe *he* couldn't.

Her eyes burning, she blinked back the unfortunate tears that were attempting to make an appearance. "Oh. Is that all? I just figured you were coming here to embarrass me by apologizing for almost—I mean, I thought—"

Joe stilled her words by resting his hand over the two she gripped together so hard that her fingertips reddened. He brushed his thumb back and forth over the back of her hand, his touch feeling so warm and comforting, even if it was only offered in kindness. She stared down at their hands because it was easier than looking into his eyes.

"Please let mc explain," Joe said. "From the beginning, I felt as if I should steer clear of you if I ever wanted to get my head on straight on the force again. I just couldn't stay away. I told myself we were only friends, even though I could feel that changing. But then, after last night and the incident at the station, I was convinced I had to put space between us, for both of our sakes."

That he continued to brush her hand with his thumb was beginning to confuse her. Shouldn't he have pulled away his hand as he was stepping back with his words? Finally, the questions were too much for her.

"Is that what you want? Space…between us?" Although her voice caught, she was surprised that she'd managed to get the question out at all.

"No, I don't."

Lindsay blinked. What was he saying? That he didn't want space, sure, but what did that mean? That his worries about the reminders she gave him weren't as significant as he'd thought? She couldn't get her hopes up when he might just be saying he wanted to stick around so he could continue to be a protective figure in Emma's life. Lifting her head, Lindsay stared into Joe's eyes. Whatever he said, she was going to take it like a woman, not a child.

"Then what *do* you want?" she asked.

"You."

"Oh." She swallowed as he lifted his free hand to her face and curled his index finger under her chin.

"And this."

He gently lifted her chin just enough, so they were looking into each other's eyes, and he leaned toward her by slow, steady steps until there was but a breath between them. Whether by instinct or need, Lindsay helped him close that last distance as her eyes fluttered shut.

Suddenly, his lips were brushing across hers in the most gentle, perfect kiss she couldn't even have predicted in her best dreams. Her first. From the *first* and *only* man she'd ever wanted to kiss her and the only one she hoped ever would.

When he pulled back, her eyes flew open in a moment of misgiving. Had her innocence been terribly obvious in her kiss? Had he decided he'd made a mistake and was bowing out now? But Joe only smiled at her and leaned in again, slanting his mouth over hers and pulling her into the sweet caress of his kiss. Her thoughts and worries fled until there was nothing and no one in her mind but this moment and this man.

Lindsay was awed and breathless when he finally eased his head away. She didn't even care that her momentous first kiss had taken place on her front porch, where everyone, neighbors and strangers alike, could have witnessed the moment without recognizing its significance. It had been a perfect moment between Joe and her, and that was all that mattered.

So this was what it felt like to be adored. Looking down at her hands, she discovered that she and Joe were still touching as they had been, only somehow their fingers had become entwined.

"Well, that was a surprise," she said, more than a little shocked that she could find any words at all.

It was a profound moment of discovery, like the sky clearing to pristine perfection following a storm, but now Lindsay had no doubt that she was in love with Joe. Why was it that her heart could so easily comprehend the truth that her mind had not been ready to see?

"A surprise?" Joe answered with a chuckle. "Not to me. Kissing you has been on my mind since I first met—well, way before I thought about it last night. Anyway, I wanted to apologize."

She was still mulling over his confession that he'd been thinking about kissing her for a while when his last comment sunk in. "Apologize? Why?" Not when all she wanted to do was to gush and *thank* him.

As she felt his grip loosen on her hand and his fingers pulling away, Lindsay was tempted to hold on tighter, but she resisted. She might not know what to expect from him, but she wouldn't allow herself to be needy now. She did have a little self-respect, after all.

"I've done things a little out of order here," Joe said with a sheepish grin. "I was supposed to take you out on a real date and impress you, and then, if I was very well-behaved, you could decide whether to let me give you a good-night kiss."

"Sounds like a pretty rigid set of rules. You have to realize our *friendship*—" she paused, unsure how to define their relationship now "—hasn't ever been by the book. Even the way we met..."

"Even so, out of order or not, I want to take you to dinner. Tonight." He nodded his head. "I mean, if you're available."

She couldn't help grinning at him. "I am, I guess."

"Wait. You never told me your news."

"Oh, that." Funny, how her shiny news had lost

some of its luster in light of recent events. "I just wanted to tell you that I'm starting to remember."

"Remember? Oh," he said, as he appeared to realize what she was talking about. An unreadable look fell across his features.

"Just a few details, but it's something."

"Well…that's great."

He didn't seem all that enthusiastic, but she didn't expect him to be after he'd once asked her if she really wanted to know those missing details. Maybe as someone who'd been there, he wished he could protect her from having to remember the things he'd seen.

Pulling his cell phone from the pocket on his belt, he tapped a button and looked at the screen. "I'd better get back to work if I plan to keep my job."

She hated to see him go, but she still had dinner tonight to look forward to. "You didn't even get anything to eat for lunch."

"I have everything I need." He reached over and rested his hand on hers again. "So I'll see you tonight, then? And if I impress you and I'm very well-behaved…"

Lindsay didn't even hesitate as she leaned in and touched her mouth to his in a tiny demonstration of the overwhelming feelings filling her heart to bursting. She could feel Joe smiling against her lips, and the sides of her mouth lifted, as well.

"Why are you kissing Trooper Joe?"

Jerking their heads apart, they both turned to find Emma standing with the glass door cracked open, staring out at them.

Joe was the first to recover. "Hey, Emma, is your movie over?"

Lindsay pulled herself to standing, using the rail, and then held her breath as she waited for her niece to answer. What if Emma asked more questions? How could she explain their relationship to a three-year-old when she and Joe hadn't even defined it yet?

But Emma only shook her head as she stepped out on the porch and let the door close. "It's not over. I'm hungry. Can we have lunch?"

Joe and Lindsay exchanged looks and then laughed.

Lindsay cleared her throat. "Lunch. I think that could be arranged."

Careful not to touch Joe as she passed him and give Emma another reason to ask questions, she rested her hand on the child's shoulder to lead her inside.

"But remember not to eat too much now," Joe said.

"Why not?" Emma wanted to know.

"The three of us are going out to dinner at six," he told her before looking up to Lindsay. "Is six okay?"

She nodded.

"And dress casual. Is pizza okay with everyone?"

"Yay! Pizza!" Emma announced.

He glanced at Lindsay, waiting on her nod. "Then six it is. One romantic dinner for three coming up."

Joe smiled that grin that still made butterflies dance in Lindsay's belly, and she knew she would be counting down the minutes until dinnertime. She wondered how she could have been so blessed to find such an amazing man, one who was more than happy to make their first date a trio outing.

She hadn't reached the point of planning the logistics of a date—who she would find to care for Emma, what she would wear, how she would do her hair—and Joe had taken care of the most important detail. Ever since she'd become Emma's guardian, she'd felt this need to handle everything, and here Joe had given her the chance to just sit back and enjoy the ride. She couldn't help feeling relief in that.

But it was more than relief. She knew it was too soon to even be tempted to think it, but Lindsay couldn't help wondering if God had special plans for her and Joe. As unlikely as it would have seemed from that first day at the Brighton Post, she was beginning to believe that God might have intended all along for them to be a family—Joe, Emma and her.

Somehow, she knew, too, that Delia would understand.

Later that night, Joe stared across the booth at the two people who, in a whirlwind of only a few weeks, had come to mean more to him than anyone else in his life. He didn't care anymore how that could have happened, how they all could have reached this point, because there was no place he would rather have been.

Sure, his misgivings were still there, scratching at the edges of a perfect picture, but he wouldn't listen to them. Not now. He wouldn't allow himself to worry about the words he still hadn't told her, either. Not tonight.

He'd made a choice to be with Lindsay. He'd chosen her and the child in her care over the career he'd once thought he loved above all things, and he understood that he would have to prepare for the fallout of that decision. Right now, though, he only wanted to think about having a great night with these two special ladies.

Lindsay looked beautiful in her jeans and a sleeveless floral blouse, with her hair falling long about her shoulders. Her soft hands were gripped together in that nervous habit of hers. Lindsay glanced up and caught her watching him, but only looked down again at those wrestling hands.

He liked that he made her nervous now, maybe as much as he had when they'd first met. The rules and boundaries had changed between them today, and whether he'd apologized or not for skewing the order of events with regard to their first kiss, he didn't want to take any of it back.

Kissing Lindsay Collins had felt like one of the most significant statements in his life, a promise he shouldn't have been making so quickly but wanted to make anyway. He also wanted to kiss her again and would have done it right now in front of the other patrons and wait staff if he wasn't worried it would shock Emma.

"How did you say you found this place?" Lindsay said, glancing around at the stark ambiance.

He grinned as he took a good look around at what she had to see. Leonetti's was just a hole-in-the-wall, mom-and-pop pizza joint, with pitted softwood booths and barely enough light to see faces across the table.

"We check out a lot of restaurants when we're out on patrol. We especially look for places that are five-oh friendly." At her questioning look, he explained, "That means they give police a discount."

"So Leonetti's passed the litmus test?"

He nodded. "That, and it has great pizza, too.

I promised you the best in Oakland County, and this is it."

"Their breadsticks are already a hit." She indicated with a nod of her head toward Emma, who was already putting away a second of a pair of fluffy sticks that the proprietor had brought as soon as they were seated.

"So, good place for a first date?" he asked.

"It's pretty good for a *first* first date." She grinned. "If I had a basis for comparison, I might be choosier."

He shook his head, still not believing. "I thought you were exaggerating about that. Oh, well. Tonight would have been a significant first date, no matter what." He indicated the child next to her with a tilt of his head.

"You mean, you don't usually take kids on your dates?"

"Well, I'd always hoped for one like that, but..." He let his words trail away as he watched Emma munching on her bread, too entranced by a football game playing on a flat-screen TV in the corner to pay any attention to the adults around her.

Anyone seeing the three of them together probably would assume that they were a family, even if Emma didn't really resemble either of them except that her eyes looked like Lindsay's. Emotion clogged his throat as he thought of other children who probably took dinners out with their parents for granted while Emma would have no memory of ordinary events like that with her mother and father. All of those memories that combined to form a happy childhood would be provided for Emma by a woman who knew little about children but had learned everything she could for her sake.

"Can we have pizza now?" Emma wanted to know as soon as she'd chewed the last bite of breadstick.

Joe sent a hopeful look toward the kitchen. "I sure hope so because if we get dinner over, we can have dessert."

Lindsay's frown turned into a grin. "Don't even think about dessert until after dinner." To Emma she added, "They probably have the pizza in the oven right now, but while we're waiting, we need to show Trooper Joe how to lose at tic-tac-toe."

She flipped over her place mat and started drawing crisscross pairs of parallel lines to set up the game. Emma hadn't quite gotten the game down yet, but she got a kick out of drawing all of those X's and O's.

By the time he'd allowed himself to be defeated three times and a large hand-tossed pepperoni had arrived, Joe had come to the conclusion that he wanted to be a part of these ordinary moments with Lindsay long-term. If he really wanted that, he needed to tell Lindsay the whole story about the accident. She might never remember more than the glimpses her memory had given her, but she deserved to know it all, no matter what it cost him.

Lindsay once would have said that he only wanted to be with her for her niece's sake because they came as a package deal, but he would have to tell her that the opposite was true now. He wanted to care for Emma because he was in love with the little girl's guardian.

Was it all happening too quickly? He couldn't help but wonder. Was he ready to take a risk like this, to race forward when he'd been content for so long just jogging in place? He'd made a mistake once before by jumping in with his heart instead of taking the time to think. Was he jumping in this time?

But as Joe's gaze met Lindsay's pale blue one across the table, his worries melted away quicker than an ice cube would have that afternoon on the sidewalk in front of Lindsay's condo. This wasn't too soon to be with Lindsay; it was the perfect time. He hadn't known what he was looking for until she'd crashed *literally* into his life and his focus had shot off in as many directions as the shards of metal and glass had that tragic night. At first, that change in his focus had seemed as awful as the accident, but things had changed. Now he wouldn't have it any other way.

Chapter Fourteen

"Look who's already back to sleep," Lindsay said several hours later as she looked over the truck's center console to the child strapped in her safety seat. Emma's tiny chin was tucked up against her chest, and her twin ponytails fell forward over her cheeks.

"I told you she'd be out for the count before we made it to the end of the street." Joe turned in the driver's seat to look into the backseat. "I wasn't expecting it before we were even out of the driveway."

He had just turned on the ignition when the two men from inside the house, one with a full head of white hair and the other whose salt-and-pepper look wasn't far behind, stepped out on the porch and waved at them.

"Look at those two." He shook his head. "You'd think they'd never met a woman before."

"You mean they're not usually big on long good-byes?" She grinned, rolling down the automatic window. "Good night, you two. Thanks, again. We had a great time."

"Don't forget, you're welcome to visit anytime," Joe's grandfather, Gino, called out.

Joe leaned across her and answered for her. "She won't, Grandpa. You've reminded her three times. Don't worry. I've got this under control."

"Make sure that you do," Leo said.

"Thanks, Dad. Good night." He shook his head as he moved back into his seat, rolling up the passenger window with the automatic control.

"They're great," Lindsay said as she watched the two men return inside the house.

"I can see how you would think so as much as they were fawning over you. They probably would have traded me off in a split second if it meant they could keep you."

"It wasn't like that." But his words still made her smile. "Anyway, I'm glad that's the place you picked to take us for dessert. Those were the best chocolate-caramel sundaes we've ever had."

Joe didn't look at her as he backed out of the driveway onto the narrow Brighton street. "You weren't so sure when we first showed up."

"I just wasn't expecting a command performance."

"You mean you don't think that meeting the

parents *and* the grandparents was a fitting end to what we both have to agree was an unusual evening?"

"It was a fitting end, all right." One that had nearly sent her into a panic attack when he'd told her just who lived in that three-bedroom ranch.

His bringing her to his father's house couldn't have had as much significance as she'd given it, but that didn't stop her from imagining the little family she, Emma and Joe would make together. Didn't stop her from dreaming.

To keep herself from starting again, Lindsay glanced to the sleeping child in the backseat. "She stole all of the Rossetti men's hearts, didn't she?"

"She wasn't the only one."

Lindsay smiled into the darkness. He always said the right things. "We probably shouldn't have stayed so late, though. We should have gone home at Emma's bedtime."

"And just have accepted defeat in Grandpa's checker tournament when you already had two kings?" He chuckled at his own joke. "Come on. Emma was fine. She went right to sleep in the guest room and didn't even ask for a second drink of water."

"I know, but she should have been in her own bed."

"You worry too much. Have I ever mentioned

that you should relax and give yourself a break sometimes?"

"A time or two."

"Well, this time I'd say Emma is doing just fine." He paused, glancing in his rearview mirror. "Except maybe for the crick in her neck from sleeping like that."

Lindsay made a sound in her throat, not convinced, but she decided to change the subject. "I liked their house. Tricia was right. Their state police room was like a museum."

"A memorial, you mean. And they're still alive."

"I thought the rest of the house looked like a celebration of family, too. There were so many pictures of you and your brother, your brother's family, plus an amazing number of your grandmother and mother."

As she pictured that long wall of photographs, she couldn't help asking, "So neither your grandpa nor your dad ever considered remarrying?"

He shook his head. "They're just a pair of merry widowers. It's part of the Rossetti men's tradition. Great marriages to women who are the loves of their lives. After my fiasco with Chelsea, I never expected to find mine."

Joe didn't say more, and he didn't look her way, but his words remained between them. Lindsay swallowed her shock. What was he saying? That he'd found someone who he thought could be his lifetime love? He couldn't be talking about her, could he?

The truck cab was quiet for the rest of the drive back to Wixom, except for the country music playing softly on the radio. Lindsay found herself resenting each mile they covered. When they reached her home, this amazing night would be over, and she didn't want it to end. Still, too soon, he pulled into her driveway.

Joe turned off the engine. "I'll carry her in."

But Lindsay rested her hand on his shoulder as he reached for the door handle.

"I wanted to thank you first for tonight," she said. "It was amazing."

"Which part? The dinner for three, the pizza or the dessert? Didn't I tell you that Leonetti's was the best?"

"All of it," she said simply because it was true. "It was the best first date I ever had."

"That isn't exactly high praise when you've had nothing to compare it to."

"True," she said, smiling. "But even if I'd been on a different first date every Friday since I was eighteen, I would still say the same thing about tonight."

"Why do you do that?" His bright teeth shone under the streetlight filtering in through the truck's rear window.

"Do what?"

"Make me want to kiss you every time you smile or laugh or say something clever. Although it was going to be tough, I'd planned to wait until I walked you to the door before taking you into my arms again so I could get this dating thing back in its proper order, but you're making my plans impossible."

"Impossible?"

Somehow, she managed not to giggle like a seventh-grader, but the nervous and giddy part she didn't have a chance of preventing. Yes, he'd kissed her earlier, but that might have been an impulse, just a reaction to all of the romantic tension that had been brewing between them for days. If he kissed her again now, then his action would involve planning and purpose. She was having a tough time sitting still, waiting for him to choose.

"Don't you think we've made enough of a front-porch scene today and given my neighbors enough fodder for backyard-fence gossip?"

"Oh." His voice was filled with disappointment, but then he turned his head sharply toward her. "Oh, you mean…"

He didn't finish whatever he'd been about to say, as instead, he leaned across the console and lifted a hand to brush his fingers through her hair.

"I've always wanted to do that," he said. "Always knew it would be that soft."

With infinite care, he tucked a strand that had

fallen forward over her cheek back behind her ear. Then he leaned even closer, until his cheek touched hers, his five o'clock shadow scratchy against her sensitive skin.

And just when she'd convinced herself he would never do it, Joe slid his arms around her, turned his head and brushed his lips over hers in the lightest whisper of a kiss. Her lids had barely fluttered closed, and he'd already lifted his head away.

She didn't even think before she reached out and slipped her arms around his neck, pulling him close again and kissing him with the kind of joy she'd never expected to experience again after her sister's death. Her mind was muddled and her lips were tingling when Joe took her by the shoulders, gently setting her back from him and leaning in to touch his forehead to hers.

"Sorry, but I'm trying very hard to be a gentleman here."

Lindsay shook her head, having to wait a few seconds for her mind to clear. "I didn't mean to—I didn't intend—"

But he only shook his head, smiling. "It's never been more important to me that I be a gentleman with anyone. It really matters this time. You matter."

"Thank you," she managed to say over the emotion filling her throat. If she hadn't already been crazy about Joe Rossetti, she would have fallen in love with him right then. No one had ever made her feel more special. "Well, I had better get her inside."

"Here. Let me help." He reached for the door again.

She shook her head. "It's not necessary. I can carry her. I can handle it. Really."

"I know you can handle it. You always could."

"Thanks." Lindsay smiled at him again. He'd helped her in more ways than he could ever know. His belief in her had helped her to believe in herself and helped her to become the kind of guardian Emma could count on.

"Just unlock your car and I'll strap her seat back in it and lock it up again," he told her.

Because she realized she wouldn't be able handle both the child and the seat, at least not in one trip, she relented. She reached in her purse and clicked the remote lock for her car. Then she touched the door handle.

"Lindsay, wait."

Feeling his touch, she looked down to see his hand on hers. She stared as he lifted her hand to his lips and kissed her knuckles, and when he lowered it, he laced their fingers together. Lindsay found herself holding her breath, not knowing whether to anticipate or dread what he was about to say.

"It's too soon for any of this," Joe began.

Lindsay drew in a breath, her heart squeezing, and she hadn't even heard him out yet. "Joe, you don't have to—"

"I know. I probably shouldn't even say it." He shook his head, still holding on to her hand. "But I have to anyway. I'm falling in love with you."

"Oh. Wow." Lindsay took several deep breaths, not sure at first she'd even heard him right. Why was it that she'd automatically braced herself for the worst, even after the wonderful day they'd spent together?

He was watching her closely. Too closely. "Well, that's one reaction, I guess. Not the one I was going for."

"I'm sorry. I just…" She paused, not knowing what else to say.

"It's okay. I'm not expecting anything. I mean I don't—*you* don't have to say anything."

He was stammering, nervous—the way he made her feel sometimes—and all she wanted to do was to make him feel confident in this one thing.

"That's just it. I do have to. I have to tell you that I love you, too."

Immediately, he crushed her to him, cradling her against his chest, her head resting against his shoulder. Feeling so warm, so safe there, encircled in his arms, Lindsay found it easy to give him the gift of her heart.

Lindsay wasn't sure whether she ever touched the ground as she climbed the steps to her condo, balancing a heavy, sleeping child against one shoulder and holding the key in her opposite hand. Joe loved her; he'd come right out and said it. And even though these feelings were new, and every bit as terrifying as they were exciting, she'd told him she loved him, too. Because she did.

She was still thinking about just how crazy she was about him while she put the key in the lock, but a ringing phone planted her feet back on the ground with an abrupt thud. Lips that had so recently been kissed pressed together in a tight line of frustration.

She pushed the door open, her stomach clenching as she caught sight of the wall clock. It was well past eleven. Her first temptation was to run and pick up the handset, but she shook her head at the thought.

"It's not going to make any difference if I get it now or ten minutes from now," she said under her breath.

She wouldn't have to check caller ID to know whose call she'd missed. Most people called on her cell instead of her landline these days, and no one else would have phoned so late at night. Instead of answering, Lindsay started up the stairs, making slow progress with her heavy load.

"Aunt Lindsay," Emma moaned, her head bobbing on Lindsay's shoulder.

"Shhh. We'll get you right back to bed, sweetie."

"The phone is ringing," the child said, her eyes halfway open.

"They'll call back." She had no doubt about that. "I just want to get you all tucked in."

They'd only made it halfway up the stairs when the phone stopped ringing. All of a sudden, her decision not to worry about it when her cell battery had died while they were still at the restaurant seemed like a bad one. She should have worried.

Flipping on the light in Emma's room, she helped her into her pajamas and dumped the laundry in the hamper before carrying her into the bathroom so Emma could brush her teeth and make a potty stop.

"I had fun tonight," Emma said, as Lindsay tucked the summer blanket up to her chin.

"Me, too, sweetie." She bent and pressed her lips to Emma's forehead.

The phone was already ringing again by the time that Lindsay made it back downstairs. She reached it by the third ring.

"Hello?"

"Lindsay Renae Collins, do you have *any* idea how late it is?" Donna said, not bothering with a greeting.

Lindsay swallowed the dread in her throat. "Yes, I know what time it is."

"I've been calling every fifteen minutes for the past four hours, and I—"

"Why were you calling?" Lindsay tried to keep the annoyance out of her voice, but even she could hear it. Her parents always checking up on her had bothered her more than she'd realized. Didn't they recognize that she was an adult who was capable of making her own decisions?

"What?" Donna paused at the interruption to her tirade. "It doesn't matter why I was calling."

"I just wondered if something was wrong."

"What's wrong is that unless your home phone *and* your cell phone have been out of service, then you've been out all night, and you've had our Emma with you. What were you thinking, keeping a three-year-old out until eleven o'clock?"

"Look, Mom. My cell died, and Joe and I were just—"

"You were with that man?" Donna's voice built with each word until the last one came out in a shriek. "That's your excuse for traipsing around with my granddaughter all night? I was ready to start calling police stations and hospitals, and you were on a date?"

Her mother made "date" sound like a nasty word. How could the best night of her life have been a bad thing? "Please, Mom, listen."

But Lindsay had already heard what her mother had said, and those words were convicting her as surely as a jury handing down a sentence. Guilt became a chill that flooded her veins. She couldn't allow herself to be annoyed with her mother for checking up on her when her parents had already lost one child. Of course her mother would panic when she couldn't get in touch with her.

"I'm sorry about the phone. Really. I'd forgotten to charge it, but I didn't think it would be a problem. Anyway, Emma had been in bed for hours at…a friend's house."

She couldn't explain why she was reticent to talk about her visit to Joe's dad's house when she'd been so pleased before that Joe had taken her to meet his family. It made no more sense than her trying to defend herself to her mother, who had no intention of listening, but she still had to try.

"Then she slept all the way home and went right back to sleep as soon as she was in her own bed," Lindsay said.

"I don't think I want to know *where* you were."

At her mother's unflattering insinuation, Lindsay gasped. Her mother must have heard it, too, because when she began again, she didn't push the suggestion farther.

"You can make all the excuses you want, but the fact remains that you continually make decisions that don't just suggest, they *announce,* that Emma isn't important to you."

"You've got to know that isn't true," Lindsay said. "Just because I went on one date—one where he happily included her—doesn't mean Emma isn't the most important person in the world to me."

Her mother clucked loudly, the way she always did when she was disappointed in her. "You are always putting your social life ahead of her, and that tells me that Emma is *not* your top priority."

"That's not fair, Mom," she said, even as questions hounded her inside. Could she say she was concentrating on Emma when she'd been busy falling in love with Joe? Hadn't her attention been divided at best? Just as Jesus said that no one could serve both God and mammon, had her divided focus not been in Emma's best interest? No, she couldn't believe that.

"You know what isn't fair?" Donna said. "That Emma lost her mother. That we lost our daughter, when that isn't the natural order of things." She'd been close to shouting by this time, but now she spoke in a quiet voice. "We should have gone first."

Emotion made Lindsay's throat burn, and her eyes flooded with tears she hadn't cried in a long time. "I'm sorry," she finally managed. "I know you've lost a lot. We all have. But I want you to know that, even though I'm dating Joe, I'm still focused on Emma. I love her, and Joe loves her, too."

Lindsay paused and then plowed forward again. "Mom, I love *him*. I feel like God has a plan for us. I think that together we might be able to build the kind of life for Emma that she deserves."

"I'm sorry, too."

"What do you mean?" Lindsay said, wondering if her mother had heard anything she'd said and if it had made any difference.

"Your father and I have decided that it will be best if we seek custody of Emma after all," she said simply. "We meet with our attorney on Monday."

Lindsay swallowed. Now she knew why her mother had called in the first place. Not entirely to check up on her. Instead, the call had been to inform her it was too late for her to prove herself.

"After all?" She wished she could control the crack in her voice, but she couldn't. "Don't appointments like that have to be set up a while in advance? How long ago did you make this decision?"

"This has been coming for some time now. You had to know that."

Lindsay had known they had concerns. She

just hadn't expected her parents would go beyond minor meddling to involve the courts.

"And you have to know this isn't what Delia would have wanted," Lindsay couldn't help saying. "She wanted me to take care of Emma. She put it in writing."

"She would have wanted someone to put her daughter first, and your father and I are prepared to do that."

Donna's significant pause made it clear she believed her daughter would never be ready for that. Lindsay's admission about her budding relationship with Joe probably only gave her more reason to doubt her.

They must have said other things after that because somehow Lindsay was lowering the phone into its cradle again, but she couldn't recall any of them. Nothing mattered after her mother's announcement that she and Lindsay's father would be taking their own daughter to court to fight for custody of their granddaughter.

Crushed didn't begin to describe how she felt, but the sense of betrayal that melded with it took her by surprise. Parents wanted their children to be happy and sacrificed for their welfare and that happiness. She'd been hearing that since Emma had first been placed in her care, and she'd learned about that sacrifice every day since.

So why didn't her own parents want *her* to

be happy? Joc wanted her to be happy, so why didn't the two people who should have loved her the most? She hated being so uncharitablc as to think it, but how could she not? If her well-being was important to them, they wouldn't have second-guessed every decision she made as Emma's guardian, questioning at every turn whether she was qualified to care for the child.

But it was more than that. If they wanted her to be happy, they wouldn't have asked her to choose between the child she adored and the man she loved. Either way, she lost, and either loss was more than she could bear.

Chapter Fifteen

Just before sunrise, Joe parked his patrol car in front of a two-story apartment building and checked the address on the laptop computer on his dashboard. Confirming he had the right place, he surveyed the scene, finding two common exits, one on either end of the building. The only other exits were the sliding-glass doors that led to porch areas on the first level and balconies on the second.

The second-floor apartment in question was among the dark ones, its vertical blinds twisted closed. But from the tip his department had received, Joe expected to find the two little boys from the Amber Alert investigation inside with the suspect. Like in so many of these cases, the suspect was the boys' noncustodial parent.

Joe itched to rush in and find out for sure, but he couldn't go in without backup, which was already en route. Rolling down his window, he waited, but he would make sure that no one made it out of the building while he did.

A squeak drew his attention back to the sliding-glass door on the second floor. The door slid open a crack.

"Stay back. I've got a gun," a man called out. The barrel of what appeared to be a .22-caliber rifle slipped out of the crack as proof that the suspect was serious.

"Hey, relax, buddy," Joe called back.

So much for waiting for backup. He would have to deal with the case the best he could and hope that someone who had his back would arrive on the scene before the situation turned ugly.

"I won't relax," the man called out. "I'm the one making demands here." With that, the suspect pulled the gun back inside and closed the door.

A knot of dread forming in his gut, Joe did a scan of the two exits. From the radio attached at his shoulder, he could hear additional units being dispatched to the scene, with each answering "I'm out," so support was on the way. Still he needed to respond now. He hoped that the desperate father hadn't injured his children already, but he didn't want to risk having the man do it while he sat there in the parking lot, either.

Reaching for the laptop, Joe typed a quick email message to dispatch. He requested a hostage negotiator and then the phone number for the apartment. The place belonged to one of the man's hunting buddies who was conveniently out of town, so he could only hope that the renter still had a landline. In an instant, he had the number. He dialed it on his cell and pushed Send.

"Lord, please give me the words, Amen," he found himself whispering, not even caring where that had come from. Those two little boys needed him to be at his best this morning, and he was ready to accept the help he needed to be just that.

The phone rang half a dozen times, suggesting the line didn't have an answering machine, before he heard the click of someone answering.

"Who is this?" the man wanted to know.

"Hey, Jared," Joe said in the most calming voice he could muster with a throat so tight. "My name is Trooper Joe Rossetti."

"How did you get this number? Did Rex call you?"

Not about to reveal the identity of the tipster, Joe just answered, "We had an idea you and the boys might be here. I thought maybe we could talk."

He sent a quick email, asking for the names of the two boys, and received another response.

"What do we have to talk about?"

Joe expected to hear another click on the line to announce his failure to connect, but the suspect only waited on the line. Like others who'd gotten themselves in bad situations, the guy needed someone to hear him out, and Joe would be that friend for now. Unless he hurt the kids. Then there would be no friend anywhere for him.

"I thought you might want to talk about Blake and Hunter. You guys have had a rough few days. The boys are still with you, aren't they?" He wanted to say "still among us," but he couldn't afford to upset Jared until he'd weighed out the situation.

"They're sleeping."

Joe swallowed. No, there hadn't been any reports of shots fired at this location, but he'd seen enough cases to know there were plenty of other ways an adult could take the life of a child. "Yeah, I guess it's pretty early for kids on summer vacation," he said with a chuckle that sounded more nervous than he'd hoped.

"They're *really* just sleeping."

"Oh. Good." Joe released the breath he'd been holding.

"You haven't done this kind of thing before, have you?" the man asked him.

"No, but could you do me a favor and not tell anybody how bad I am at it? That would be bad for my rep."

"Your secret is safe with me. It's Joe, right?"

"Yeah."

"Do you have kids?"

"No, none yet."

"Kids are great. You'll find out someday."

Joe wondered how much more he should tell, but this conversation seemed to be keeping the suspect calm, and that was what he had to do until the negotiator arrived. From the radio traffic, he could tell that other units were in the vicinity, but they were coming in silent. He only had to hold on a little longer.

"My girlfriend has a little girl," he heard himself saying. It was the first time he'd called Lindsay his girlfriend, and he liked the sound of it. "When I marry her, I'll be an instant father." He hadn't said any of this aloud yet, either, but he found in admitting his plans to a stranger how comfortable he was with the decision.

"Well, get ready because fatherhood's a powerful thing. You'll find that you'll do almost anything for that little person who looks up at you like you're a hero."

Joe could hear the smile in the other man's voice, so he realized it was time to change the subject. "Then, Jared, why all of this?"

The man made an anguished sound. "My ex, she got custody, and she married this new jerk, and she keeps the boys away from me. My boys!"

"That has to be rough, but do you really think this is the solution?"

"It seemed like a good one at the time. Now? Not so much."

Joe straightened in his seat. He was close to making this work. "So what's with the gun?"

"Hunting rifle," Jared said with a chuckle. "Not even loaded. Can't have a loaded gun around kids, you know. You need to remember that in your line of work."

"Thank you, God," Joe whispered before speaking into the cell again. "Any chance I could get you to put that gun out on the balcony and close the slider? Oh, are there any other weapons inside?"

By the time the other patrol cars had pulled in next to his, Joe had Jared cuffed and was putting him into the car. The boys had slept through the whole event and were found curled together in a big guest bed. Joe had already called in social services to pick them up and return them to their mother.

He hated knowing that Jared was facing jail time and wouldn't be seeing his sons again for an even longer time, but Joe hoped his testimony might help the guy receive a lighter sentence.

The rest of his shift dragged, as he couldn't wait to get over to Lindsay's to tell her about the morning's events. Joe was excited to tell her that he had his edge back, but it was more than that.

He wanted her to know that she was right and that he was grateful to her for helping him to see that he wasn't in control.

If his meeting Lindsay and their falling in love weren't reasons enough to convince him that God had always been in control, then this morning's events were a good reminder. God was always there to carry him, especially through life's rough spots, and Joe was finally ready to let Him.

A scream followed Lindsay that night as she clawed her way out of her dream. She clasped a hand over her mouth to make it stop.

She blinked out into the darkness that took on familiar shapes just as it had the night before. Why was this happening again? Would she and Emma both suffer from regular nightmares now? Would she even be able to be there for Emma's bad dreams now that her parents were planning to take the child away?

Emma. Lindsay's gaze shot to the open doorway. Had the scream awakened her niece? She waited for the sounds of crying or padding feet in the hall. But the house was silent. Had it even been an audible scream, or had all of that piercing sound been inside her mind?

This dream wasn't like the night before, though, when the images had traveled back with her to consciousness with disturbing clarity. She couldn't even remember what had frightened her and made her call out in the night. She didn't want to know, but maybe it was time that she did.

Stretching to the bedside table, she flipped on the lamp. Then, in the safety of its illumination, she closed her eyes and tried to recall the images from her dream the other night. They returned as they had before—the sights, the smells, an unconscious Delia, even the light on the windshield.

But this time the driver's-side door opened in her memory. It was Joe who leaned in with rain dripping off the brim of his state trooper's hat. He glanced at Lindsay and pressed two fingers to Delia's throat before he unbuckled Lindsay's safety belt and started pulling her from the car.

Then she heard a desperate voice in her head and realized with a shock that it was hers. "Please. Please. Help...my sister...first."

Lindsay hadn't been able to get a word in from the time that Joe showed up at her condo after his shift, so she'd just let him inside and allowed him to talk. What she had to say could wait a little while, but not forever, and although she dreaded being the one to say it, it had to be said.

"You wouldn't believe it." Joe was pacing around the room in his excitement. "Pretty soon I had formed this connection with him, and we were talking about kids and…things, and I was convincing him to let me take him into custody."

"Sounds amazing."

Her voice sounded flat in her ears, but he must have missed it because he kept on going.

"I'm no longer a liability on the force, and it's all because of you," he told her. "You always trusted God, no matter what, and you showed me how I can trust Him, too. I don't have to feel as if I'm carrying the whole world on my shoulders anymore. I can just do my best and be assured that He'll take care of the rest."

"That's great, Joe."

"I even remembered one of those memory verses that you're always talking about. Luke 1:37, 'For with God nothing will be impossible.'"

"Don't give me the credit."

This time, either her words or her tone must have struck him as odd because Joe stopped and turned to study her. She was perched on the arm of the sofa, too restless to sit down, but he bent to look at her more closely.

"What's going on, Lindsay? Have you been crying?"

It must have been obvious that she had been because he barely paused before peppering her with questions.

"Did something happen to you? Is it Emma? Does it have something to do with your parents?"

Because her distress had so many layers, each with more acute pain than the layer above it, Lindsay was surprised that Joe had been able to key in to so many of them. Still, she shook her head in answer to his questions. She couldn't tell him about her pain over the custody battle when she felt betrayed by him, as well.

"Where is Emma?"

"She was tired when I picked her up from day care, so I put her down for a nap."

He gave her a strange look that told her he remembered her worrying about giving the child late-afternoon naps before, but he didn't say anything.

"Then tell me what it is," he said finally. "What has you so upset?"

Slowly, she looked up at him and stared hard at him, hoping he felt as trapped by the truth as she did. "I remembered."

"What do you mean?" he asked, though the cautious look in his eyes suggested that he might have an idea.

"I had another dream last night, and then I remembered." She took a deep breath and then said that last, all-important word. "Everything."

"Oh." His Adam's apple shifted.

"That's all you have to say? *Oh?*"

Squeezing his eyes shut, Joe rubbed his temples.

When he opened his eyes again, he bent in front of her and tried to take her hands. "Let me explain."

Lindsay jumped up, grabbed her cane and stalked away from him—anything to avoid his touch. "It's too little, too late, don't you think?"

He followed after her. "I'm so—"

She turned back to him, cutting him off. "I don't want to hear that you're sorry. Not now." Fury and hurt became a powerful combination, causing her hands to shake as she paced. "When were you going to tell me that I asked you—no, begged you—to save Delia first? But you didn't listen. Did you just hope I would never remember?"

He opened his mouth as if to try to answer her, but she was too worked up to give him the chance.

"How could you not tell me? I deserved to know the truth. The whole truth. Isn't that the message all you law-enforcement types try to sell from the witness stand?" She shook her head hard to push the pain away, but it still clung to her with the same intensity that her injuries once had. "You were wrong to keep it from me."

Joe released a long sigh and stepped aside to allow her to pace. "I know it was. It's just that I didn't know how—"

"I knew it, too. I knew there was something you weren't telling me." She folded her arms and glared back at him. "I kept thinking the accident was partially my fault or something, and you'd altered the police record for me since I was the only survivor."

"So you thought I was either a bad cop who would falsify police reports, or a loser with a hero complex who would do anything to protect you." He chuckled, but he didn't smile.

"It's not funny."

"I know."

Joe swallowed, sensing that his next words would be every bit as critical to their relationship as his conversation with the suspect that morning had been to the well-being of two little boys. He stalled by walking to the window and staring outside for several seconds before turning back to her.

"I really am sorry." He cleared his throat. "You have to believe that. At first I didn't think you were ready to hear the whole story. Your own subconscious was trying to shield you from it, so I tried, too. It happened just as I told you it did. I just didn't think you needed a reminder of your plea that I couldn't honor."

Lindsay didn't exactly leap away from him then, but Joe sensed her stepping back from him in her stiff posture and the tight flex of her jaw. He wished there was a way he could have told her that would have hurt less, but that had been the case all along, and that was why they were in this situation now.

"You should have told me then," Lindsay said, "but even if you didn't, that doesn't change the fact that there were dozens of other times when you could have told me."

"I wanted to, believe me," he said, holding his hands wide. "I knew I owed it to you. But it never seemed to be a right time. The more time I spent with you, and the more time I wanted to be with you, the harder it became to tell you."

But she was shaking her head. "If you'd wanted to tell me, you would have found the right time."

He nodded because she was right. "And then I fell in love with you. I knew it was too late to tell you without taking the risk that I would lose you." He shook his head as the thought of it tore at his heart. "I couldn't take the risk."

"Then you were almost right."

Joe blinked. "What? What do you mean?"

"You *have* lost me, but because you *didn't* tell me."

His insides clenching, he started toward her, shaking his head. "No. No, Lindsay. You can't mean that."

But her eyes flashed anger. "Yes, I mean it. You couldn't trust me with the truth about my own life. You made me wait until I remembered it and let me relive it like a nightmare."

"I'm so sorry. I was wrong. But can't you forgive me?" He reached out to her again, resting his hands on her forearms. "We can get past this."

"No!" She shook her head and backed out of his reach, losing her balance but regaining it by hitting her hand on the wall. "You shouldn't have done it."

And just like that, Joe's fear of losing Lindsay turned to a fury at least as strong as what she had to be feeling.

"Which thing, Lindsay? Which thing shouldn't I have done? Saved you first or failed to tell you that awful other part of the story?" The words felt like acid on his tongue, but he spoke them anyway because he needed to hear the answer.

"Both," she said in a quiet, resigned voice.

"You can't mean that." Although he'd guessed she felt that way, he was still shocked by the tragedy of hearing her say it aloud.

"I shouldn't have become involved with you in the first place." She shook her head. "You're the man who chose between Delia and me. Even after I begged you to help her."

Joe stalked to the window again, wondering whether he should just keep on walking or turn and offer at least a parting battle, though the war was already lost. But hopeless or not, he couldn't leave until he'd had his say.

"Your parents were wrong to ever let you be-

lieve that you weren't as valuable as your sister."
When he saw her open her mouth to argue with
him, he shook his head to stop her. "But do you
know what's worse than that? It's that you never
realized your parents were wrong."

"You don't know anything about it."

"Don't I?"

She shook her head, but she wouldn't look up
at him.

"I might not know everything, but these things I
do know. You are valuable, a child of God, worthy
of being loved." He paused to watch her, not convinced she was even listening to him, but he had
to try.

"You are even worth being the person someone
pulls from an accident *first*," he told her. "That's
in the tragic circumstance that your rescuer can't
save you both."

"Are you finished?" she said in a small voice.

He shook his head. "No. I don't think that I
am. Because I love you. You weren't being honest
when you said you loved me. You were looking
for a reason to sabotage our relationship because
you don't believe you deserve to be loved."

"That's not true," she began, but she stopped
when he shook his head.

"You'll never be able to love anyone until you
learn to love yourself."

With that, he turned away from her and started

for the door. He didn't stop until he was all the way to his truck. He couldn't allow himself to look back at her, to even think about what he was leaving behind, because that would only make it harder for him to leave. She didn't want him, and there was nothing he could do to change that.

But no matter what he'd said or neglected to say to her, no matter what he'd thought before this moment, he knew without a doubt that he'd left a part of his heart that he would never find again in that condo with Lindsay. He would survive; he didn't have any choice. But he would never love again. Some scars ran deeper than the ones on Lindsay's skin. His sliced straight through his heart.

Chapter Sixteen

Lindsay stared after Joe's truck as he pulled out from the curb and headed down the street. He didn't look her way, and his brake lights never flashed to signal second thoughts. She knew he was mad, but she, not he, was justified in being so angry that she couldn't see straight. So angry that her eyes burned and her chest felt ready to implode.

Crossing the room to sit on the tan sofa by the window, she hugged one of the red decorative pillows to her chest. She continued to stare as though his truck might come roaring down the street again. He wasn't coming back, and she shouldn't even want him to.

How could he ever have justified not telling her the whole truth from the night of the accident? His excuse that he'd been worried that she hadn't been ready to hear it had been just that…an excuse. But it was worse than that. Instead of falling all over her with apologies the way any rational person would have, Joe had turned the whole thing on her, as if it had been *her fault* that he'd kept the truth from her.

How could he have said all of those things about her parents and especially about her, someone he *claimed* to love? Though angry, she was hurt even more, as much by the cruel things he'd said as by the fact that he'd told her he loved her while he'd still been hiding part of the truth from her.

Joe was wrong to say she didn't love herself. He had to be. He was wrong to believe she couldn't love someone else, too, because she was certain that she really did love him. Even now that a relationship between them would be impossible, her heart still cried out for him.

He was the one person she wanted to tell about the custody crisis over Emma, the only one who would understand how much losing the child would destroy her. Now she would have no one in her corner when she faced her parents in court.

"Are you crying?"

Lindsay turned around with a start, the pillow still braced against her chest. Emma stood in the doorway, her ponytails sticking up every which way after her brief nap. How long had she been standing there? Lindsay had been staring so hard out the window, pretending not to care one way or another whether Joe came back, that she hadn't noticed Emma coming down the stairs.

"Of course not, honey." But when Lindsay brushed her hands over her face, they came away damp with tears. When had that happened? She shook her head. "Oh. It's nothing."

"Where is Trooper Joe?"

She cleared her throat. "He's gone now."

Emma frowned. "When is he coming back?"

"I don't know." She reached out her arms so the child would come and sit on her lap. "How did you know he was here?"

"I heard you talking. You were loud."

Lindsay straightened. At least Emma hadn't said she'd heard them fighting because that was exactly what they'd been doing. And all of a sudden Lindsay couldn't swallow for the knot in her throat. She'd just had one of those experiences that parents dread—that their children will overhear them fighting with their spouses. Not only would Joe never be her spouse, but also, Emma would probably never legally be her child. It was too much. How could she bear to lose both of them?

"Can we go riding?"

Even in her sadness, Lindsay couldn't help smiling at the question. *Riding* was what Emma had started calling the few times that they'd gone for a run with the jogging stroller since the child didn't do any of it on foot.

"You know, that sounds like a good idea."

In that other life before the accident, Lindsay used to go running when she needed to think, and thinking was something she really needed to do today. "You like riding, don't you?"

"You do, too."

Lindsay nodded. Running this way was just another one of the changes that had come into their lives since she and Emma had become a family, one that she would miss terribly if the child couldn't live with her anymore.

After a quick clothes change and a slathering on of sunscreen, Lindsay strapped Emma into the jogging stroller, and they started up her street toward the bike trail. The rhythmic clicks of Lindsay's running shoes on the pavement calmed her nerves as they always had. As her muscles and lungs burned with exertion, she found her anger against Joe beginning to cool.

She was still mad at him—she wasn't ready to let go of her righteous indignation just yet—but she could begin to see that Joe had been holding back information because he'd wanted to protect her from more pain.

She couldn't help wondering if some of the things he'd said were true. Had she used her anger over his withholding the truth as an excuse to sabotage their relationship? And if she really loved herself, then why had she been willing to settle for living in Delia's shadow? And why hadn't she insisted to her parents that there was more to her than what they seemed to see?

Glancing down as she continued her slow and steady progress forward, Lindsay caught sight of Emma sitting awkwardly in the seat, with her back arched and her head tilted so she could stare up at Lindsay through the lenses of her princess sunglasses.

"You're running fast," the child observed.

"Getting faster, I guess," Lindsay answered, surprised she was barely winded.

It couldn't have been more obvious in the way that Emma looked up at Lindsay that she adored her. Emma didn't mind that her aunt hadn't had a clue about what to do with a child when she suddenly found one living with her. None of her mistakes or missteps mattered to the child who simply loved her.

"God don't make junk," she whispered, remembering the poster wisdom that Delia used to say to her with a wink after they'd endured another of their parents' awkward comparisons.

Had she ever believed her sister's words back then? And then Joe had reminded her today that she was a child of God and worthy of love. Did she really believe she was? The truth accused and convicted her without deliberation.

Earlier, Joe had given her the credit for being his inspiration to repair his relationship with God. But how could she claim to have a strong faith when she'd had so little value for one of God's creations—herself?

"Aunt Lindsay?"

"I'll run faster again in a minute, honey, okay?"

"Okay." She was quiet for a few seconds before saying again in a small voice, "Aunt Lindsay?"

"What, honey?" She looked down this time and found the child watching her too closely.

"Will you be my mommy for always now?"

Suddenly unable to draw in enough oxygen to support her stride, Lindsay slowed to a stop and took several long breaths to calm herself before she could speak. "Emma, your mommy will always be your mommy, even if she's gone to Heaven, just like your daddy will always be your daddy."

"Then can you be my Mommy Lindsay?"

"I don't know, but I'll always be your Aunt Lindsay. I will always love you." Her heart ached that she couldn't even guarantee she would play a significant role in her niece's life, any more than she could assure Emma that they would be living together a month from now.

It wasn't enough. Lindsay owed Emma more

than just acceptance that she couldn't win a custody battle against her parents. Still, she was relieved that the little girl accepted what she told her now, even smiling up at her. But just when Lindsay put her hands back on the handlebar and started forward again, Emma asked another question.

"Are you going to marry Trooper Joe? He could be my Daddy Joe."

"What?"

It was all Lindsay could do not to burst into tears again. As questions bombarded her thoughts, Lindsay continued to push the jogger forward but stared down at the child. Just how much had her niece overheard? But then she remembered that Emma had not only caught her and Joe kissing on the front porch just a day before, but she'd also been a part of that amazing first and last date.

"I'm sorry, but I don't think that's going to happen."

"Okay."

Something about Emma's easy acceptance of that sad reality didn't sit well with Lindsay. Especially since Lindsay had resigned herself to it easily enough for the both of them. She'd barely given him a chance to say he was sorry, and she hadn't accepted his apology.

She'd been no better when she'd found out about her parents' plan to seek custody. She'd only listened, feeling helpless, when she should have challenged what she'd heard. Didn't she have any fight in her at all? Not only had she lost the only man she could ever love, now she also would lose the child who had become the center of her life. She felt hopeless and alone.

Lindsay's heart was heavy as she walked the rest of the way to the condo. After she let Emma in the door and the child ran upstairs to play in her room, Lindsay went to find her purse on the desk area in the kitchen. From the outside zipper compartment, she pulled out that folded and worn piece of paper that had come to mean so much to her.

Taking a seat at the dinette, she unfolded the paper and read those familiar words from an anonymous author.

"Don't be afraid.
You are a child of God.
You are precious in His eyes.
He counts every hair on your head.

"Don't be afraid.
God knows your pain.
He sees your doubts and fears.
He wants to heal your broken heart.

"Don't be afraid.
You are not alone.

God will wipe away your tears.
He'll cradle you in His loving arms."

Tears came in a rush before she had time to put a dam in place. Dampness even dotted the paper that Joe had given her to remind her to trust God during some of her darkest days. He couldn't possibly have known that those same words would comfort her after she'd made the mistake of sending him away.

She read the words she could have recited by heart one more time, and then she folded her hands and bowed her head, closing her eyes.

"Father, I've made a mess of everything, as usual," she prayed. "Please help me to make it right. I'm placing the situation in Your hands. Please guide me if it is Your will. Amen."

As she lifted her head, Lindsay felt an urge to fight with the kind of intensity she'd never felt before. For Emma. For herself. For a future with Joe. No matter what had happened between them today, she knew if she asked Joe to help her deal with her parents, he would. But not this time. She needed to handle this situation on her own. She didn't need someone to save her, only to love her.

The prospect of it would have terrified her a few months ago, but she was no longer that person. Just as her leg had become stronger in the healing process, allowing her to nearly give up the cane, *she* was stronger. Maybe it was because Joe had helped her to see the strength she already possessed, or maybe she'd never had anything worth fighting for before.

"'Do not go gentle into that good night.'" Lindsay smiled as she got up from the table and started for the stairs. Joe would find it ironic that she'd started quoting poets like Dylan Thomas along with her Bible verses, but just as in that poem Thomas had encouraged his father to "rage" against impending death, she intended to fight for the people who made her life worth living.

After making a quick call, she climbed the stairs and crossed to Emma's room. The child sat in the middle of the floor, dressing fashion dolls in outrageous outfits.

"Hey, sweetie. How would you like to go and play with Miss Tricia and Mr. Brett's kids for a little while?"

She didn't have to ask twice. Emma dumped her fashion dolls unceremoniously in the toy box, grabbed Monkey Man and started putting on her shoes.

Soon they were on their way to Milford for a quick child-care stop, and then Lindsay would continue on, alone, toward a destination she'd needed to reach for a long time. Although she was still waiting for God's will here, she'd learned that prayer was most effective with a little action.

God had a plan, which she hoped He would reveal to her soon, but she knew in her heart that whatever happened now, they all would be safe in His arms.

Lindsay sat on the edge of her father's worn leather easy chair and faced her parents sitting opposite her on the sofa. She'd expected the words to pour from her with ease, but now she searched madly for a place to begin. Her parents weren't any help, watching her with their arms crossed over their chests.

"Mom, Dad, I came here because I wanted to talk to you about Emma."

"Where is she, anyway?" her mother wanted to know.

"I already told you that a friend, Tricia, is watching her." She paused, trying to pick just the right words. "So here's what I've come to say. I don't want to you to go to court to seek custody of Emma. She needs to stay with me, always."

Her mother opened her mouth to interrupt, but her father rested his hand on hers to stop her.

"Let's give Lindsay her say."

Lindsay cleared her throat. "I might never measure up to your memory of Delia. Who am I kidding? I never measured up to my sister, even when we were still teenagers. But the fact remains that Delia chose me to care for her daughter.

"I don't know why she chose me. Maybe she saw some value in me," she paused, flicking a glance their way before looking down at her hands. "Something my parents couldn't see. Maybe she thought I would be the kind of guardian—the kind of parent—who would celebrate Emma's accomplishments no matter what they were and love her for just being her."

She looked at her own parents steadily. "She was right. I will."

Finding it too difficult to stay seated, Lindsay stood and started pacing the room filled with photographs and memories, some with bright smiles, some with curling edges. She didn't use her cane now, but her movements were slow and steady.

"Even if I'm not the best guardian for Emma yet, I intend to become the kind of parent that she deserves." She turned back to the couple still sitting on the couch, their eyes wide in reaction to her words. "I love you both, but if you take me to court for custody, I will fight you. I have to."

"Lindsay, you need to think about Emma," Donna said.

"I am, Mom, and I'm thinking about myself, as well. Raising Emma is going to be the best thing I ever do, and I'm going to do it my way," she said. "I also plan to keep seeing Joe. I'll even marry him if he asks. Emma loves him, and he'll make a good father figure for her."

Warming to her subject, she returned to her seat. "I'll probably make other decisions in raising Emma that you won't agree with, either. I might make her bedtime too late or let her eat junk food on occasion or even put her down to sleep a few hours at my future father-in-law's house and then take her home—"

"Future what?" Brian wanted to know.

"Never mind, Dad. But like when Delia was raising her own daughter, those decisions regarding Emma will be entirely up to me."

Out of words, Lindsay stopped. There was nothing like squeezing a lifetime of conversations into a single, painful talk. But some words did change everything, and whether happily or tragically, this one has one of them. So she folded her hands and waited to find out which way this one would go.

"I'm sorry, Lindsay."

At her father's opening words, Lindsay braced herself. She'd promised a fight, and now she had to prepare herself to deliver on that promise.

"I'm sorry, too," her mother said. "For everything."

Lindsay blinked. "I don't understand."

"No, we were the ones who never understood," Brian said. "We never even realized that we were showing favoritism to Delia or that our comparisons caused you so much pain. We're blessed that you still love us at all."

"Of course I love you. You're my parents."

Donna shook her head. "I'm beginning to see why Delia picked you to raise her daughter. You're determined and loyal, almost to a fault. You're just the person who has many things to teach our granddaughter."

"You're right about that." Brian patted his wife's arm and then turned back to his daughter. "We thought if we kept Emma close to us, it would be like having Delia with us."

"That makes sense," Lindsay said. "Emma is part of her, and we'll always want to keep her memory alive. Just leave her with me, and you can see her anytime you want."

Her parents looked at each other and back at Lindsay. Her father spoke for the both of them. "We won't proceed with plans to file for custody. Now tell us more about this young man of yours."

"Any other time I would talk your ear off, but I've really messed up with Joe, and I need to work things out with him first. If that's even possible."

"Relax, honey," Donna told her daughter as she moved to the door. "If our daughter could forgive us for all we've done, then anything that's broken can be fixed."

Chapter Seventeen

Joe grumbled as he pulled his patrol car to a stop outside the guard shack at Kensington Metropark. The guard waved him past. Clara had probably just been trying to annoy him when she'd suggested that he make a pass through the almost-fifteen-hundred-acre park during his shift that afternoon, so he'd been surprised when Brett had agreed with her and had made it an order.

Okay, he'd been testy the past few days, but that didn't mean that they needed to gang up on him and send him on the family reunion beat.

He hadn't driven far when he passed the first few reunions. Banners for the Long and Kryzewski families staked their claims in prime spots near one of the playgrounds and a baseball field. He could just imagine what a Rossetti reunion would be like: pretty light on the female side of the family, but there would definitely be a nice patrol car as a centerpiece.

He didn't want to think about the person he would want there, sharing his name, sharing his life. He'd chosen to avoid lost causes, and he and Lindsay together had every sign of being one of those. Loving her hadn't made her love him enough to forgive him, so his hoping and praying for it was unlikely to bring her back to him.

Clara had mentioned something about him patrolling the area near the beach changing rooms, where there had been vandalism lately. It would have been nice if she'd told him which beach, but since he was going to have to do a drive-by of both, he followed the signs to Martindale Beach first. He didn't even want to think about why he would have chosen that one first, but he pressed his lips together when he caught sight of the waterpark they'd never had the chance to visit.

The beach was more crowded this time, with cars filling most of the parking spaces, so instead of just driving by, Joe parked his car and took a walk out toward the beach. Past the changing room, he scanned the grassy area in the foreground, with the long stretch of sand and the green-gray water just beyond.

Nothing appeared out of the ordinary, just sunbathers dotting the sand, laughing kids bobbing in the water and weekend volleyball players showing off their skills at the net. Oh, and one family that had planned a reunion in an unfortunate location, too close to the beach.

Joe glanced at the family's banner that looked far more like a poster made with felt-tip markers, but when he read the name, he had to do a double take. Rossetti?

Fully aware that Rossetti was a rare surname this side of the Atlantic and even more aware that his dad and grandpa weren't much for party planning, Joe took a closer look. What he saw took his breath away. In what had to be the smallest reunion in the history of family reunions, the two ladies that meant the world to him sat on a blanket spread on the grass. They were having a private picnic.

Emma glanced at him first and jumped up, waving. Lindsay looked up, too, but her smile was a cautious one. Unlike the rest of the beach bathers, the two of them looked more like attendees at a church picnic in floral sundresses. Although Emma's hair was tied up in her trademark ponytails, Lindsay wore hers long, with the breeze lifting some of those pretty red tresses. Clearly, Lindsay had fussed and prepared for this meeting. What he didn't know was why.

Clara and Brett had set him up. Of that he was certain. The rest he wasn't sure about at all. What did all of this mean? Had Lindsay forgiven him? Could he forgive her for pushing him away? Oh, who was he kidding? He'd forgiven her the minute he'd driven away from her home, even though he'd been nursing a broken heart.

Joe was tempted to run across the grassy area to reach them like a soupy tissue commercial, but he didn't yet know why they were there. Besides, a police officer running in uniform probably would set off panic on the beach, so he forced himself to slow. He needed to be cautious, anyway. The risk of being hurt again was too great.

But as was the case since he'd met her, the pull of this amazing woman was stronger than his ability to resist, even for his own good.

At the edge of the blanket, he stopped. "What's all of this about?"

Lindsay glanced around at the containers of fried chicken, veggies, potato salad, coleslaw, watermelon and cookies. "I guess we did overdo it a little."

She indicated the farthest container. "The cookies were Emma's idea."

"That's because she has great taste," he said.

"Sit down, Trooper Joe." Already, Emma had his hand and was pulling him to the blanket.

He let Lindsay stall for as long as he could as she served up plates for three and they all started eating, but finally he couldn't take anymore. "You didn't answer my question. Rossetti?" He pointed to the sign.

"How else would you have found us here?" As she answered him, she pulled a hand-held video game from her pocket and handed it to Emma. The child accepted it, popped the earphones on and started clicking buttons while continuing to eat.

"Do you think all of those people are wondering whether Emma and I are getting arrested for being too dressed up at the beach?" She looked left and right, indicating the spectators who were watching them.

"I think a citation might be in order," he said with a smile. "But you still didn't..." Joe held his hands wide.

"Fine. I wanted to tell you I talked to my parents."

"Oh." He hoped he didn't sound as disappointed as he felt. "And you enlisted both Clara and Brett to bring me here so you could tell me that?"

"It wasn't hard to convince them to help."

"I see," he said. "So, was your visit with your parents a good thing?"

"No, it was great. I couldn't tell you before because I was so upset about...the other thing...but my parents were meeting with an attorney to sue for custody of Emma."

"That's awful."

"It's okay though," she said with a smile. "I told them how I felt, and I talked them out of it. They even apologized for showing favoritism to Delia."

As she relayed the story, Lindsay lit up with self-confidence that had always seemed to be missing before. As much as Joe hated that he hadn't known about her crisis, hadn't been able to be there for her, he couldn't help but to celebrate with her. She'd stood up for herself and for Emma, but that didn't mean she was ready to stand up for a relationship with him.

Joe took a bite of chicken as Lindsay continued telling the details of her happy story, but her next comment had him choking on his food.

"I also told them I planned to marry you…" she paused as if only then realizing what she'd said "…if you asked me, that is."

For several seconds he could only cough into his napkin, but he finally got the spasms under control.

Lindsay shook her head. "I'm sorry about that. It had to be a bit much. We only went on one date, and I'm new at all of this stuff. I'm so sorry about overreacting about the accident scene. I understand that you were trying to shield me from more pain when you didn't tell me everything about that night."

"I was," he said simply. He couldn't believe his

ears. She nodded as if she really believed him this time.

She continued, "I know I have some scars, but I also know I love you. I'm surer of that than I've been of anything in my whole life.

"I've probably been in love with you since I realized that you were the one who gave me that poem that told me to trust God when you weren't even ready to do that yourself."

She glanced lovingly at the child, who was playing her game, oblivious of their conversation, and then she looked over at him again. "I realize it's a lot to ask a man to take on a woman and a child who come as a package deal, but I know you would be wonderful for Emma. And for me."

Lindsay stared at Joe, shocked and dazed by the things she'd said. Had all of those things really just come from her mouth? Was it good for anyone to ever be that honest? She turned to watch Emma again, worried that she might have messed up their future with the man who was surely supposed to be part of it, by pushing too hard, too fast.

She hadn't even asked him if he'd forgiven her for pushing *him* away before. If he couldn't forgive her, what would she do then?

As a movement in her peripheral vision caught her attention, Lindsay turned back to see Joe kneeling before her on both knees, uniform and all. A knot formed in her throat as she stared into his eyes and waited for him to say words that would change both of their lives.

With gentle hands, he reached for both of hers. "Lindsay, I love you. You turned my life upside down the day you came into it, and I wouldn't take back my perfectly balanced life for anything in the world. There's only one thing I can think of that would be better than making you my wife, and that's helping to raise Emma as part of a package deal.

"If you don't already have plans, would you mind spending every day, for the rest of your life, with me?" He smiled. "Will you marry me?"

"Hmm, let me think about it." She took a bite of watermelon and thoughtfully chewed and swallowed, but finally she grinned back at him. "Yes. I thought you'd never ask."

He didn't hesitate, but leaned forward and drew her into his arms. His kiss felt like a promise of a lifetime filled with more laughter than tears, more hope than regrets. She answered with a promise of her own.

She didn't know how long the kiss went on, hoped it would never end, but at the sound of applause, they drew quickly away from each other and looked around to the crowd they'd drawn. The ruckus must have pulled Emma out of her video counting game because she squeezed between them and was looking out with trepidation at the crowd of strangers.

"I think we're going to have to work on this whole public-kissing thing," Lindsay said as she pulled back, still holding Emma to her side.

"Are you kidding? I don't care who sees me kiss the woman I love. We just stand out because I'm the only guy on the beach in uniform."

As she shifted Emma onto her lap, Lindsay scanned the curious faces around her. "Do you think they know?"

"That we're engaged? They know. There might not be a ring yet. I didn't know you'd be giving my future in-laws the scoop so early, so I wasn't prepared. But with the whole kneeling thing, oh yeah, they know. I want them all to know."

With a squirming preschooler hugged between them, Joe bent his head to brush his lips across Lindsay's again. She didn't care that a bunch of sunbathers were watching because it was a perfect moment, full of promise and dreams for the future. A future for three individuals who soon would be a real family.

Lindsay brushed her hands over the smooth satin of her tea-length bridal gown, feeling the crush of the tulle from the layers beneath. As she lifted her hands, she was startled by the sparkle of the bridal set on her finger, proving that all of this was real, not just an amazing dream.

The day had been too perfect for them to have planned it in less than a month, but her mother had come through with the surprising skills of drill sergeant and professional wedding planner combined into one. Donna had rolled with it, even when Lindsay had announced that she wanted to have the service at the Milford church instead of their home church. Forgiveness had come easily for her family, when combined with love and understanding.

"What are you smiling about, Mrs. Rossetti?"

Joe grinned back at her as he hurried back into the church vestibule, pulling Emma, whose dress was a miniature and baby-blue copy of Lindsay's, by the hand. She wondered why he'd been so fast to volunteer when a certain flower girl had needed someone to take her for a potty break before they started the receiving line, but a suspiciously loosened bow tie gave her a hint. Even with the loosened tie, Joe still looked like he could have been on the cover of a bridal magazine. He was right here with her, instead.

"'Mrs. Rossetti.' I like the sound of that."

"Well, you'd better because you're stuck with it." He took her hand with his free one. "And me."

"Aunt Lindsay, where's my basket? I lost my basket."

"I don't know, honey. Let me— " As Lindsay

glanced around for a missing basket for flowers, she noticed that another bouquet was conspicuously absent as well. "Hey, where are my—"

"Flowers?" Dressed in a simple, baby-blue dress, Tricia came through the door from the sanctuary then, carrying both the missing basket and Lindsay's amazing bouquet of white roses, along with her own bridesmaid's nosegay.

"You were so excited to have tied the knot with your man that you forgot your flowers and nearly dragged him out of the church," Tricia said.

She handed the basket back to Emma and then gave Lindsay her bouquet.

"Oh, no, Tricia. You've got it all wrong," Joe said. "I was the excited one. I was dragging *her* out of the church. You know how much we guys *love* weddings."

"That's why we Rossetti men only go through the whole ceremony thing once."

They all looked back to find Joe's father, Leo, leading his own father through the door from the sanctuary. Nobody mentioned that Leo had brought Clara to the wedding as his date, but several of them exchanged secret smiles.

"Okay, everyone, take your places," Lindsay's mother called out as soon as the usher led her into the vestibule.

But instead of stepping into the line herself,

Donna hurried over and hugged her daughter. "You make a beautiful bride, Lindsay."

"I only wish Delia could have been here." Tears that had danced in Lindsay's eyes several times throughout the ceremony spilled over her lower lids this time.

"Oh, she's here." Donna brushed away a tear at the corner of her eye. "She's looking down on us from Heaven today, and she's got to be so proud of you and pleased with the man you chose. I know *we* are."

Lindsay hugged her mother a second time, and then brushed away her tears to get ready to greet their guests.

"Hey, I haven't had the chance to kiss the bride." Brian corrected that mistake by quickly bussing his daughter and then moving on to shake his son-in-law's hand.

"Sir, I promise to take very good care of your daughter and your granddaughter," Joe said, with a serious expression.

Brian grinned. "Oh, I don't have any doubt about that. Our daughter has a good head on her shoulders. We're certain she has chosen well. And don't kid yourself about taking care of her. She'll be taking care of you, too."

As the members of the bridal party stepped back, taking their places in the receiving line, Joe turned to his bride. "This really happened, didn't it?"

"Oh yeah. Are you sorry?"

"How could I be sorry when I've just been blessed with the two best things I never knew I wanted? You don't ever have to give me a gift from now on because you can't top this."

He leaned in and brushed his lips sweetly across hers.

"I want a kiss, too," Emma said.

He reached down and lifted Emma into his arms, and her guardians pressed kisses to both of her cheeks.

As he lowered the child back to the ground, Lindsay couldn't help watching Joe. It wasn't so long ago that he'd carried her from the accident, and now she carried him in her heart. As two people who'd known the tragedy of loss and the fleeting quality of life, they realized that a love like theirs was precious and rare. They were clinging to it with all their might. They would face the future together—just Joe and Lindsay and Emma…hand in hand in hand.

* * * * *

Dear Reader,

If you're like me, sometimes you look in the mirror and see imperfections. I find myself thinking, "If only this were a little smaller or smoother." Even away from the mirror, I sometimes wish that I had better math or time-management skills. I have to be reminded that I am a child of God, created in His image, and that as a Christian I should love all of His creations. Myself included.

I explored this idea in *Safe in His Arms*. Lindsay Collins has no trouble putting her trust in God, but she has a much more difficult time loving herself. Before she can find a lifetime love, she must learn that she is precious to God and worthy of love. I like the words in the beginning of Genesis 1:31a: "And God saw everything that he had made and behold it was very good." If God sees such value in His creations, then shouldn't we learn to appreciate ourselves, imperfections included?

I love hearing from readers and may be contacted through my website, www.danacorbit. com, or through regular mail at P.O. Box 2251, Farmington Hills, MI 48333-2251 or friend me on Facebook.

Dana Corbit

Questions for Discussion

1. As Lindsay searches for answers to fill the blanks in her memory over her tragic accident, her mother suggests that some stones are better left unturned. Are there times when we are really better off not knowing the whole truth? Or is the truth vital, no matter how painful? Why or why not?

2. Lindsay's parents worry that she won't be a good guardian for Emma. What are some of the qualities necessary to be a good guardian for someone else's child, and which of these qualities does Lindsay possess?

3. Joe and Lindsay share the experience of growing up with high expectations from their families. How did they respond differently to those expectations? How did your parents' expectations mold your development, and how have yours affected your children?

4. Lindsay insists that the poem Joe carried in his state trooper's hat and left with her at the hospital was a sign that he hadn't lost his faith. What do you think the poem says about the man who carried it around with him?

5. Why does Lindsay believe Joe should have pulled Delia from the wreckage first? What are your thoughts on society placing more value on specific victims, such as young parents over other adults?

6. Lindsay feels guilty over her attraction to Joe Rossetti because she wonders if it might be a betrayal of her sister's memory. Are her feelings justified? What are some ways that she could get past those feelings?

7. The symbolism of Lindsay being safe in Joe's arms and all of us finding safety in the Father's arms is central to this story. Have you ever experienced a tough time in your life when you felt safe knowing that God was carrying you?

8. For Joe, the accident involving Lindsay and her sister was the night he lost his edge as a police officer. How might a police officer who questions his reactions and second-guesses his decisions be a danger to himself or the public?

9. Lindsay mourns the loss of her sister and her personal freedom, but she feels guilty because she misses running, as well. Why would the loss of that activity be so important to Lindsay? Have you ever mourned the

loss of an activity you were passionate about when you had to give it up?

10. Lindsay believes her faith is strong, and yet she has a difficult time loving herself. Can a person really love God with all her heart and yet not love herself as one of His creations?

11. Why does Lindsay suspect that Joe is hiding something about the accident? If you were Lindsay, which would you find harder to forgive, the stark truth or that Joe kept part of that truth from you?

12. Why is it so significant that Joe brings Lindsay to meet his friends Brett and Tricia? Describe the first time you introduced your future spouse to your friends. Was that meeting or the meeting with your parents more difficult?

13. Lindsay has grown up with the favoritism her parents showed to her sister, and she must address that pain with her parents as she proves she is the best guardian for Emma. Do you agree with how she approaches her parents? How would you have handled it differently?

14. Though Lindsay constantly worries about making mistakes as she cares for Emma, Joe

encourages her to give herself a break. Which things are more important in parenting—schedules and rules or time and effort?

15. Joe questions whether a loving God would have allowed him and Emma to grow up without their mothers and why He would have allowed tragedies to take place. Is it okay for Christians to question God? How do you justify those types of tragedies in your mind?

Love Inspired®
SUSPENSE
RIVETING INSPIRATIONAL ROMANCE

Watch for our series of edge-
of-your-seat suspense novels.
These contemporary tales
of intrigue and romance
feature Christian characters
facing challenges to their faith...
and their lives!

AVAILABLE IN REGULAR
& LARGER-PRINT FORMATS

For exciting stories that reflect traditional values,
visit:
www.ReaderService.com